LUCKY
BROKEN
GIRL

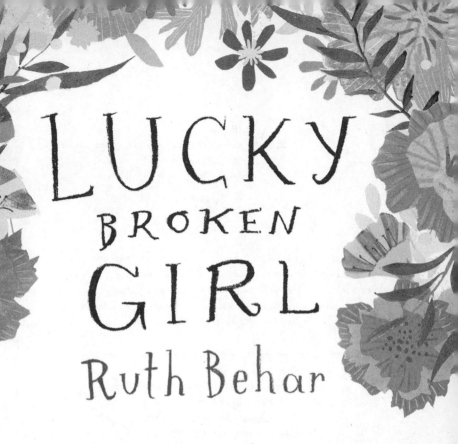

LUCKY
BROKEN
GIRL

Ruth Behar

 Nancy Paulsen Books

Nancy Paulsen Books
an imprint of Penguin Random House LLC
375 Hudson Street
New York, NY 10014

Library of Congress Cataloging-in-Publication Data
Names: Behar, Ruth, 1956– author.
Title: Lucky broken girl / Ruth Behar.
Description: New York, NY : Nancy Paulsen Books, [2017]
Summary: In 1960s New York, fifth-grader Ruthie, a Cuban-Jewish immigrant, must rely on books, art,
her family, and friends in her multicultural neighborhood when an accident puts her in a body cast.
Identifiers: LCCN 2016022378 | ISBN 9780399546440 (hardback)
Subjects: | CYAC: Fractures—Fiction. | Family life—New York (State)—New York—Fiction. |
Immigrants—Fiction. | Cuban Americans—Fiction. | Neighbors—Fiction. | Queens (New York, N.Y.)—
History—20th century—Fiction. | BISAC: JUVENILE FICTION / People & Places / United States /
Hispanic & Latino. | JUVENILE FICTION / Health & Daily Living / Diseases, Illnesses & Injuries. |
JUVENILE FICTION / Social Issues / Emotions & Feelings.
Classification: LCC PZ7.1.B447 Luc 2017 | DDC [Fic]—dc23
LC record available at https://lccn.loc.gov/2016022378

Printed in the United States of America.
ISBN 9780399546440
5 7 9 10 8 6

Design by Marikka Tamura.
Text set in Maxime Std.

For my son, Gabriel,
who was also wounded as a child and recovered,
and for children everywhere who suffer and look for hope

CONTENTS

PART I

MISS HOPSCOTCH QUEEN OF QUEENS

I am not dumb

When we lived in Cuba, I was smart. But when we got to Queens, in New York City, in the United States of America, I became dumb, just because I couldn't speak English.

So I got put in the dumb class in fifth grade at P.S. 117. It's the class for the *bobos*, the kids who failed at math and reading. Also in it are the kids the teachers call "delinquents." They come to school late and talk back and are always chewing gum. Even though they're considered the bad kids, most of them are nice to me. "Here, Ruthie, have some Chiclets!" they whisper and pass me a handful.

We aren't supposed to chew gum in school, so we hold the Chiclets in our mouths until we go outside for recess. Then we chew the Chiclets to death and stick the gook on the bottom of our desks when we come back inside.

Most of the kids know I'm in this class because I'm from another country, not because I really belong there. Or maybe I do belong there? It's been eight months since school started and our teacher promised I wouldn't be in the class for long.

1

I am not dumb. I am not dumb. I am not dumb . . .

The first time I worked up the courage to raise my hand in class was a few weeks after we had arrived from Cuba and I was wearing flip-flops instead of shoes and socks like the other kids. But when our teacher, Mrs. Sarota, called on me to answer the math problem, I didn't have the words to say the number in English.

"Well, Ruth?" she asked, staring down at my bare feet. "Do you know the answer or not?"

I froze and a few kids laughed at me. But not Ramu.

He's not dumb either. Ramu is in our class because he's also from a different country. He comes from India and was raised there by his grandmother, who only speaks a language called Bengali. His parents came to New York first, and after they made enough money, they brought Ramu and his little brother, Avik, here.

Ramu has picked up English faster than I have because his parents know English and force him to speak it at home. Mine are always yelling, *"¡Habla en español!"* Especially Mami, who can understand a little English, but is usually too embarrassed to try to speak it.

Ramu is skinny and bows his head when anyone talks to him. I'm his only friend and that's because he lives down the hall from us on the sixth floor of our apartment building. Ramu brings Avik to school and I bring my brother, Izzie. Our little brothers are in the same kindergarten class. But after school Ramu and Avik rush straight home. Mrs. Sharma doesn't let them play with the other children.

Their apartment smells different from ours. I get whiffs

of it whenever we stumble into each other on the way to school. Today when Ramu and Avik stepped into the hall, Izzie and I were waiting for the elevator, and I asked, "What is that perfume?"

"It's my mother's curry," Ramu says.

"What's curry?"

"A spice. It makes everything taste good, even cauliflower."

"That's amazing."

"Yes, it is. And my mother burns sandalwood incense. She says it's good for meditation and the spirits like it too."

"Spirits?"

"People who used to be alive, when they're not alive anymore, become spirits. My grandmother says they are all around us. We can't see them but they watch over us. Of course, spirits don't eat, but they can smell fragrant things like curry and incense."

During lunch at the cafeteria, Ramu offers me something from his lunch box, a pastry filled with mashed potatoes his mother made.

"It's a samosa," Ramu tells me. "Maybe you'll find it too spicy."

Some kids at the table pretend to hold their noses. One says, "It smells like sweaty armpits!"

"No it doesn't!" I shout back.

I take a slow first bite. It tastes like a *papa rellena*, a crispy stuffed potato my nanny Caro made for me as a snack in Cuba. Eating Ramu's samosa makes me feel like Caro and Cuba aren't so far away.

"It's real good! Thanks, Ramu."

3

Ramu gives me a shy smile. "Very glad you like it."

I beg Mami to make *pastelitos de guayaba* after Izzie and I get home. The following day, I give Ramu one of the sweet pastries at lunch.

"The filling is guava fruit. I hope you'll like it," I tell him.

Ramu eats it slowly without saying a word. When he's done, he finally says, "I like guavas. We have them in India too," and I sigh.

"And do you have mangos in India?"

"Oh yes, drippy sweet mangos."

"Just like in Cuba!"

"I don't just miss the mangos," Ramu says. "I miss being able to go outside and play with friends. My mother worries too much about us. She doesn't let us do anything by ourselves."

"I know what you mean. In Cuba, even when I was five years old, my mother used to let me take a taxi all by myself to go visit my aunt Zoila, who used to sew pretty dresses for me. Can you imagine?"

"Yes, here everything is different," he says, with a faraway look in his eyes.

"But maybe one day we'll both get to taste mangos in India and Cuba!" I say, trying to cheer him up.

"Oh, Ruthie, I like that you have such an imagination!"

Ramu and I sit together every afternoon after lunch period so we can practice our English.

Our favorite story is "The Princess Who Could Not Cry," about a princess who is placed under an evil spell and forgets

4

how to cry. She laughs at everything, even sad things. When they toss away all the toys she loves from the tallest tower of the castle, she laughs, even though she feels terrible.

A little ragged girl arrives and announces, "I've come to help the princess cry."

The queen tells her, "Promise me you won't hurt my daughter."

The little ragged girl curtsies and replies, "I promise, Your Majesty, I will bring no harm upon your daughter. I just want to help her."

She goes into a room with the princess and draws two onions out of her bag.

"Let's peel these onions," the little ragged girl tells the princess.

As the little ragged girl and the princess pull apart the layers of the onions, the tears start pouring from both their eyes.

That is how the princess learns to cry!

The evil spell is broken, and the little ragged girl and her poor mother are given a nice house next to the castle where they live happily ever after.

"That is the best story!" I say to Ramu as we finish reading aloud.

"Yes, it's very fine," he replies. "Very fine indeed."

"Ramu, you always talk such a fancy English."

"Like they do in England. It's the Queen's English, you see."

"Yes! And now we live in Queens!" I say, joking.

"Very charming, Ruthie. That's almost funny."

"Let's ask Mrs. Sarota to test us!" I tell Ramu.

"But will you ask her, Ruthie, please? You see, in India, we don't talk to the teacher unless the teacher talks to us."

"Okay, I will ask. I'm not afraid of the teacher."

Mrs. Sarota comes to our desk and I say, "Me and Ramu are ready to switch into the smart class."

"In English, we say 'Ramu and I.' 'Me and Ramu' is incorrect."

I don't lose my courage. I repeat, "Ramu and I are ready to switch into the smart class."

"Is that so, young lady? Both of you?"

"Yeah, Mrs. Sarota," I reply, trying to keep from giggling. Mrs. Sarota wears her hair in a big bird nest on top of her head and today it's lopsided.

"Very well, young lady. Which of you can spell the word 'commiserate'?"

Ramu gets it wrong, but I get it right—two *M*s and only one *S*.

She doesn't ask, but I also know what the word means. To "commiserate" is to feel sorry for somebody else's bad luck.

"Very good, Ruth. I agree you're ready to be promoted. But remember to say 'yes' rather than 'yeah.' On Monday, you can join the regular fifth-grade class."

I see Ramu gazing sadly toward the floor. It's not fair. He's much better at English than I am. He talks like the Queen of England herself.

"Please, Mrs. Sarota, can you give Ramu another chance? Give him a harder word and see if he can spell it. Please."

Mrs. Sarota's eyes suddenly sparkle. "You said the magic word, 'please.' Ramu, can you spell the word 'souvenir'?"

I would have gotten that word wrong, but Ramu knows how to spell it right.

"Excellent job, Ramu. You are also promoted," Mrs. Sarota says. "On Monday, you and Ruth can join the regular fifth-grade class."

"Mrs. Sarota, you are very kind," Ramu says in his most polite voice.

Ramu gives me one of his shy smiles and that is enough of a thank-you for me.

I knew I wasn't dumb. I knew Ramu wasn't dumb either.

It's Friday. After the weekend, when we come back to school, both of us will be in our new class with the smart kids.

Yippee!

I collect my schoolbooks and say good-bye to the other kids. One of them looks sad that I'm leaving and gives me some Chiclets. "You may need them!"

I wish all the kids could come with Ramu and me to the smart class. I don't think any of them are really dumb. They just find school boring. They'd rather play all day.

In a chorus they call out, "Bye, Ruthie! Bye! Study hard or they'll send you back here again!"

go-go boots

The buildings on our street are made of old bricks and they all look exactly the same. If you don't know the number of your building, you're lost. My brother, Izzie, and I know our building by now, but we still walk home together from school, holding hands, as if we'd got to New York only yesterday.

The lawns have gone from snowy white to blotchy brown to a hopeful green color, and dandelions are sprouting on them. I wish I could run barefoot in the grass the way I did in Havana. There was a park nearby that had giant banyan trees that you could lie under and curly grass that tickled your toes when you ran through it. But most of the lawns here have wire fences around them that will cut your fingers if you touch them and signs that say "Keep Off the Grass!"

We are near our building when a girl named Danielle calls out, "Ruthie, Ruthie," and catches up with us.

Danielle is from Belgium and acts very sophisticated. She has silky black hair that reaches to her shoulders and flips perfectly. She looks like she could be on TV. With my messy ponytails and dress from the bargain basement, I feel like the fairy tale's ragged girl with the basket of onions when I'm around Miss Mademoiselle Danielle. Today she has on a lace-trimmed beige blouse and a pleated blue skirt. And she's wearing new go-go boots. Black go-go boots! She also just arrived in New York, but they put her in the smart class because she speaks French *and* English.

"Do you want to play hopscotch?" Danielle says.

"Yeah," I reply. "I always want to play."

"Très bien," she says and smiles. Danielle crosses the street, walking so elegantly in her black go-go boots to a building as drab and dreary as ours. Before she disappears, she turns and waves. "See you out here in a minute!"

Izzie and I race each other to see who gets into the elevator first. I get there a second before him and press the button for the sixth floor, and as the door closes, we are panting and breathless. We can't wait to change out of our school clothes and go out and play. We have the whole weekend. No school till Monday.

Yippee!

As soon as we step into our apartment, I can smell the sweet rose scent of Mami's Maja soap, which comes wrapped in tissue paper with a picture of a Spanish flamenco dancer in a red-and-black gown, and Papi's Old Spice, which he splashes on his cheeks before going to work.

Mami is waiting for us at the door and gives us a hug and a kiss. She always looks so pretty, as if she's going to a party. She's wearing her clothes from Cuba—a polka-dot dress with buttons down the front and a wide leather belt—and she's got her high heels on, and red lipstick. "A wife has to look her best when her husband comes home," she always says.

"Mami, you got lipstick on me!" Izzie yells, wiping the stain off his cheek.

"I'm sorry, *mi niño*. It's just that I'm always so happy to see you," she tells us in Spanish.

Mami points to the dining table, set with two grilled cheese sandwiches and two glasses of chocolate milk.

"We just want to go out and play!" Izzie complains.

"If you don't eat, you'll faint," Mami tells him. *"Se van a desmayar."*

We gobble up our sandwiches and chug down our milk while Mami stands over us trying to get us to slow down. *"¡Niños, no se apuren tanto!"*

But nothing can keep Izzie and me locked up in the house while the sun is shining. We jump up from our seats, change into our play clothes, and rush to the door. I remember to grab some chalk and toss it into my jacket pocket.

Mami stops us and reminds us not to be home late. Our hands must be clean and we must be smiling and ready to kiss Papi the minute he walks in the door or he gets angry.

Off we go, finally!

Izzie says, "I'll race you! I'll run down the stairs and you take the elevator!"

"Okay, Izzie! Let's see who gets there first."

Sure enough, Izzie gets to the first floor just as the elevator door opens.

"Wow, you did it, Izzie!"

My little brother looks so proud of himself. He's cute with his crooked bangs and missing front teeth.

"Now let's see if I can beat the other boys at tag. They're really fast," he says, sounding worried.

"You will, Izzie, you will."

And he scurries off to "the back," an alleyway behind our row of buildings where the boys chase each other for hours and hours.

Blue and pink chalk in hand, I claim the sidewalk in front of our building for my hopscotch board. I bend down to sketch out the squares for the game and add flowers at the four corners.

When I look up from drawing, Danielle is there.

"What a pretty hopscotch you're making, Ruthie!"

Danielle is still looking so stylish in her fancy school clothes. Isn't she worried she'll get them dirty? Won't her mother scold her then? But what makes me the most jealous is that Danielle is still wearing her black go-go boots! And I have on my old sneakers, with the holes forming around my big toes.

I've been begging Mami for a pair of go-go boots ever since seeing the blond lady on TV wearing them and singing that song "These Boots Are Made for Walkin'." And I can't stop humming that catchy song:

These boots are made for walkin'
And that's just what they'll do

One of these days these boots
Are gonna walk all over you!

Now Danielle, looking so grown-up in her black go-go boots, announces, "I'll go first!"

Ava and June, who live in the building next door, come to play with us. They are plain American girls. They only speak English. They never dream about a lost beautiful island. They are surprised when they hear me talking Spanish with Mami.

"Why do you talk another language?" they ask me.

"Because we're from Cuba, that's why."

"Oh," they reply, and don't know what else to say.

They stare at Danielle as she hops from square to square on the hopscotch in her go-go boots, light as air.

I'm not light like Danielle, but I am strong, and I get two squares farther up on the hopscotch.

Danielle doesn't mind at all. She smiles and says, "Very nice, Ruthie! You are excellent at hopscotch! You are Miss Hopscotch Queen of Queens!"

She says the word "hopscotch," extending the *shhhh* sound at the end of the word with a French accent and it sounds glamorous.

Ava and June take turns after Danielle and me. The four of us keep on playing one round after another. I can throw the stone farther and leap higher than Danielle, Ava, and June. Yes, yes! I am Miss Hopscotch Queen of Queens! Yippee!

We don't stop playing until the sky grows dark and loses all its blueness.

I'm happy being Miss Hopscotch Queen of Queens.

But I still wish I had go-go boots.

"Guess what, Danielle," I say.

"What, Ruthie?"

"I'm moving to your class on Monday."

"Really? *C'est magnifique!*"

Those words just roll off Danielle's tongue. Then she glances at her watch. She's the only girl I know who wears a watch and the wristband is a gleaming gold bracelet.

"Excuse me, my friends, I must go. My mother is expecting me for dinner."

She skips away in her black go-go boots and halfway down the block she turns around and smiles at me and says, "Bye, *chérie*, bye, bye."

stop crying about Cuba

When Mami sees me all sweaty from playing hopscotch, she shakes her head.

"Ruti, wash your face and hands, and put on a clean dress. Then come help me with dinner."

"Danielle wore her nice clothes to play hopscotch and she had on new go-go boots!"

Mami frowns and says, "*Mi niña*, don't start that again. You know we can't afford go-go boots." Mami is always reminding me how hard Papi works to pay the rent.

We just have one bedroom in our apartment, and Mami and Papi gave it to Izzie and me. They got a Castro convertible sofa for themselves that doubles as a bed. Every night Mami pulls open the sofa and makes the bed, tucking the sheets into the wire frame that scratches her hands. And every morning, she turns it back into a sofa, folding it up like an accordion. She sighs when she opens and closes the sofa.

Mami misses Cuba, where we had an apartment with two bedrooms and a balcony that looked out at the ocean and let in the breezes and the sunshine. She misses standing

14

on the balcony and lowering the basket down with a rope for the peddler to fill with pineapples and coconuts. She misses the people, who smile at you in the street, even if they don't know who you are. And she misses the tall palm trees that tickle the sky. Now she and Papi have to sleep in an uncomfortable sofa called Castro, the name of the man who stole their country from them.

Sometimes Mami's sadness gets so bad she can't hold back her tears, but she mostly cries when Papi isn't home. He gets angry when she cries. I want to hear Mami laugh again like she used to when we lived in Cuba.

In the bedroom I notice my rag doll is missing. She usually sits on my bed, on top of my pillow.

I run back to the kitchen. "Mami, where's my doll from Cuba?"

"It was falling apart. Didn't you notice the stuffing had come out and was getting all over everything?"

"But where is it?"

"I threw it in the garbage."

"Mami, why? That was my doll from Cuba."

"We'll get you a new doll when we have a little money. Now hurry up and get changed so you can help me."

"Mami, that was so mean! You should have asked me first."

I knew I was getting too old to go to sleep cuddling a doll, but with her in my arms I felt that Cuba wasn't so far away. Now she is gone and I feel like I could cry. But I want to be strong, not weak and sad like Mami, so I try to cheer myself up.

I decide to put on my frilly dress that has layers of lace. It's the dress I wore when we left Cuba a year ago.

I dig around in the closet but can't find it.

"Mami, where's my dress from Cuba?"

"I gave that dress to Sylvia, so your cousin Lily can get some use out of it."

"But that was my favorite dress!" I scream.

"Don't yell at me! And don't be selfish. You know that dress didn't fit you anymore."

"That's not true! I could squeeze into it. I just had to hold my breath."

"You kept tearing the seams and I got tired of stitching them back together."

"Mami, why are you taking away all my things from Cuba?"

I feel the tears trying to come out of my eyes. But I make them stop.

"Ruti, stop arguing. You're wasting time. Papi will be here any minute. Dinner has to be ready when he comes in the door."

Mami has cooked a big pot of *arroz con pollo*, the rice yellow and soupy with pieces of chicken mixed in. She scoops it out spoonful by spoonful and creates a huge mound on a long oval platter.

She sees me watching her and reaches over and hugs me. "Ruti, I'm sorry I threw out your doll and gave away your dress from Cuba. But I'm trying to forget Cuba. Do you understand?"

"I guess, Mami." I sigh.

Even when Mami does something wrong, I can't stay angry with her for long because I feel sorry for her. That big word I had to spell today to get out of the dumb class is how I feel about Mami. I am always trying to commiserate with her.

"Can I decorate the *arroz con pollo*?"

"*Sí, mi niña.*"

I take slices of red pepper Mami has roasted in the oven and green peas from a Green Giant can and arrange them on the mound of *arroz con pollo*. I create swirls with the peppers and circles with the peas.

As I am finishing up, Izzie walks in with his clothes all caked with mud.

"Hurry and wash your face and change out of those filthy clothes before Papi arrives!" Mami says.

We are always afraid of upsetting Papi. So it's a big surprise when Papi comes home with a smile on his face. He's been to the barbershop and had his curly hair and thick mustache trimmed. What is that he's carrying? It's a shopping bag . . .

"For you, Ruti."

A gift—for me! A box—could it be?

Yes! White go-go boots!

They fit just right.

"*¡Gracias, Papi, gracias!*"

I give him a kiss on the cheek.

He asks me to give him a hug too.

I give him a hug and say, "I love the boots, Papi. But didn't they have black ones?"

Papi says, "Black go-go boots are for grown-up *señoras*. You're a good girl. White boots are better for a good girl. Promise me you'll always be a good girl."

"*¡Sí, Papi, sí!*"

Papi pulls a small package out of his suit pocket. "And this is for Izzie."

Izzie is so happy he rips opens the package. Inside is a Matchbox toy car, a blue Cadillac. Izzie adores playing with cars. He jumps into Papi's arms and yells, "*¡Gracias, Papi, gracias!*" and kisses Papi's cheek.

"I'm glad you like the car, *mi niño*, but don't kiss me, okay? You can kiss your mami but not your papi. Men don't kiss each other. Men shake hands."

Papi's good mood makes everything at home much better.

I love my go-go boots! I decide the white boots are nicer, after all. I wish I could run outside in the night and dance around in them. Because they are white boots, they would glow in the dark like two moons. I can't wait to show them off to Danielle, Ava, and June, and all the girls at school.

"Can I wear my go-go boots now, Papi? While we eat dinner?"

"Go ahead, *mi niña*. Enjoy them," Papi says, loosening his tie and taking his seat at the head of the table.

I cross my legs under the table and feel the left boot greeting the right boot. My boots have heels! Leaning back in my chair, my feet now touch the floor. And that makes me feel very grown-up.

We aren't very religious, but today Mami bought a challah.

Papi recites the Hebrew blessing and then he tears a piece of bread for each of us and says, "We are lucky to live in a free country and have this bread to eat."

Mami brings out the *arroz con pollo* from the kitchen.

"Look, Papi, I decorated it!"

"*Muy bien*, Ruti, *muy bien*. I'm glad you're helping your mother."

Mami serves Papi first, then me and Izzie, and herself last.

But Papi won't eat. He looks disappointed at the food on his plate.

"Rebequita, *mi amor*, isn't there a chicken breast you could give me?"

"No chicken breasts today. I got drumsticks. They were cheaper."

"But you know I don't like dark meat."

"I'm sorry, I thought that mixed in with the rice you would like it."

"I'll just eat the rice."

"Alberto, I don't want to say this, but Ruti didn't need a pair of boots right now. May is almost here. And Izzie has plenty of toy cars."

That's all it takes for Papi's temper to flare. He slams his fist on the table and yells, "Who are you to question my decisions? I am the man in this house! I earn the money and I can spend it as I please. You said our daughter dreamed of owning go-go boots, so I got them for her. And our little boy loves cars and I think that's good."

"I'm sorry, I can't do anything right," Mami replies in a voice so small it fades away.

I feel bad for Mami, but I don't want to give up my go-go boots. I jump up and say, "Wait! I have an idea!" I rush to the bedroom and come back with my piggy bank. It's stuffed with pennies. "Here, look! I have money."

"Put that away," Papi says gruffly. "Enough talk of money."

We finish our dinner in silence. Mami, Izzie, and I eat everything on our plates. Papi angrily picks his way through the *arroz con pollo*, pushing the pieces of chicken to the edge of his plate.

As she tiptoes around Papi clearing the table, Mami says, "I invited the family over for dessert. They'll be here soon."

"You should have asked me first," Papi replies. "What if I don't feel like seeing anyone right now?"

But it's too late. The doorbell rings and there are my grandparents, Baba and Zeide. Behind them are Aunt Sylvia and Uncle Bill, who was born in the Bronx and we call *el americano*. And my cousins Dennis and Lily, who are twins and the same age as Izzie, and just as wild as him.

Baba and Zeide live on the third floor. Sylvia, Bill, Dennis, and Lily live on the fourth floor. They don't have to travel far to visit us!

"*¿Todos quieren un cafecito?*" Mami asks, her eyes lighting up.

All the grown-ups say yes.

Mami serves the Cuban coffee in tiny cups that look like toy cups. We children can't have any Cuban coffee. It's too strong.

"*Delicioso*, Rebeca," says Uncle Bill with his thick American accent.

20

Zeide reaches into his suit pocket and pulls out four Tootsie Rolls. He always carries candies in his pocket for us.

"*¿Quieren caramelos, kinderle?*" he asks us. Zeide was born in Russia and he mixes Spanish and Yiddish when he talks.

We all say yes and each take a Tootsie Roll from the palms of his large hands and give Zeide a hug.

Mami serves everyone thick slices of her gooey flan. The topping is made of burned sugar that tastes sweet and also a little bitter.

"*Hermanita*, you make the best flan of anyone I know," Aunt Sylvia says in English, so Uncle Bill and Dennis and Lily understand, since they don't speak Spanish. Then she adds, "*Muy rico.*"

Mami smiles her sad smile. "Not as good as the flan I used to make in Cuba. The sugar isn't the same here. And the milk is so watery."

Baba doesn't like it when Mami complains. "Listen to me, *mi hija*, the flan is just as good as in Cuba. Let's forget we ever lived there," she says in Spanish. Then, to show off her English that she's learning in night school, she adds, "My darling daughter, she needs to understand it is necessary to go forward, not back."

Uncle Bill, with his booming voice, says, "Aren't you glad you're in a free country?"

Papi shakes his head and sighs. He tries to speak English but mixes Spanish in. "My wife *no sabe* appreciate that she can complain all she wants because she's in America. *Este es un país libre*, the best country in the world."

Mami wipes her tears with her embroidered Cuban

handkerchief that I think is too beautiful to soil with her sadness.

I try to make things better by saying, "Guess what! Look! I have new go-go boots!"

"They're so beautiful, Ruthie!" Lily says and turns to Aunt Sylvia. "Mommy, Mommy, I want boots just like Ruthie's!"

"You're too little for boots like that," Aunt Sylvia says. "You're only five years old. Wait till you're older. Maybe Ruti will give you her boots when she outgrows them, like she gives you her dresses." Aunt Sylvia winks at me. "Ruti, will you, when they're too small for you?"

"I will, I promise! And I'll take good care of them, so they'll be good as new. Okay, Lily?"

Lily nods. "I guess so. But I want to grow up fast."

"You will, sweetie," says Uncle Bill. "Faster than you can sing 'Skip to My Lou.'"

Then I remember I haven't shared my good news.

"Mami, Papi, Uncle Bill, Aunt Sylvia, Baba, Zeide! Guess what! I've been promoted to the smart class! I'll start on Monday. Isn't that great?"

"Very good, Ruthie," Uncle Bill says. "You're really picking up English."

"The teacher tested me with a hard word to spell—'commiserate.' And I got it right!"

"That is a hard word. Do you know what it means?" Uncle Bill asks.

"It means to feel sorry for someone else's bad luck."

"That's right, Ruthie. You are a heck of a lucky girl. You

are lucky your parents brought you to America. Study hard and you'll go far in this country."

"Thank you, Uncle Bill."

"Don't thank me, honey. Thank your father for bringing you here."

I look at Papi, who is nodding and smiling.

Then I look at Mami. Her eyes are lowered. I want to commiserate with her like I always do, but I think Papi and Uncle Bill are right. It's time for Mami to stop crying about Cuba.

I go to Mami and put my arms around her. As I'm hugging her, I reach over and pull the handkerchief out of her hand.

"Mami, will you give this *pañuelo* to me? I don't have my doll or my frilly dress anymore. I want to have something to remember Cuba."

She whispers to me in Spanish, "Keep it, *mi niña*, keep it. We will both try to forget about Cuba. We're in America now. No more tears, *mi niña*. Just a bright happy future."

I see Mami smile and swallow her tears. I just hope we can live up to her brave words.

poco a poco

I beg Mami to let me go to bed wearing my go-go boots.
But she says no.

The minute I wake up, though, I slip them on. Still in my
pajamas, I sing:

> *These boots are made for walkin'*
> *And that's just what they'll do.*
> *One of these days these boots*
> *Are gonna walk all over you!*

Like the blonde on TV, I swing my arms and dance around.

> *Are you ready, boots?*

I climb onto my bed and stand tall in my boots on top of
the sheets. I jump up and down. Then I jump as high as I can
and leap to the ground, landing on my feet.

Izzie comes in and yells, "What are you doing, Roofie?
I'm going to tell Mami!"

"Shhh, don't say anything."

I show him that the bed is still clean because the boots are brand-new.

"I'm learning to dance in my boots. One day I'll be famous. I'll be on TV!"

"You're nuts, Roofie." He makes the crazy sign with his finger.

"No, I'm not! I'm happy! Happy, happy, happy!"

"Come have breakfast!" Mami calls from the kitchen.

Papi has already left for work. On Saturdays, he has a second job fumigating apartments in Spanish Harlem.

Izzie and I eat our eggs and toast quickly, so we can run outside and play.

I put the dirty dishes in the sink and Mami stops me as I grab my chalk.

"Izzie can go play. But I need you to do the grocery shopping with me."

"But why do I have to help and not Izzie?"

"Because you're older. And you're a girl. That's why. Now take off those boots. They cost a lot of money. You can't be wearing them every day."

"That's not fair!"

"Do as I say. Please, Ruti."

Mami looks at me with her sad eyes and I give in. I place my go-go boots in their box and put on my old sneakers.

It's a sunny day, so we walk all the way down the hill to Queens Boulevard instead of taking the bus. I drag the shopping cart behind me, slowing my pace so I can walk along with Mami, who is wearing her high heels. There are lots of cracks in the sidewalks and she has to be careful not to trip in her high heels. But Mami always wears heels. She says she's so short she doesn't want the entire world looking down at her.

I leap over the cracks, pretending I'm playing hopscotch. I sing the tune the kids in my class taught me:

> *Step on a crack,*
> *Break your mother's back.*

I look over at Mami, thankful she doesn't know enough English to understand.

At Dan's Supermarket, Mami asks me to translate into Spanish the labels of everything she sees for sale on the shelves. What's the difference between regular milk and skim milk? What's a Salisbury steak? How do you cook a TV dinner? Why don't they have coconut ice cream?

Finally we bring all our groceries to the checkout lane. The cashier is a bald man with yellow eyes who stares at Mami as if she's for sale too.

"I see you got Cap'n Crunch, little lady. Good choice! It's my favorite cereal," he says.

Mami can't understand what the man is saying. She turns to me to translate for her.

"Dice que es un cereal muy bueno," I explain to Mami.

The man licks his lips. "You are *mucho bonita*, missus."

I see Mami's hands are shaking. She looks frightened, like

she wants to run away. I reach into her wallet and hand the money to the man.

"*Ya*, Mami, *vamos,*" I say.

I grab hold of Mami's hand as if she were a little girl lost in the woods. With the other hand, I grab hold of the shopping cart and push it out the door as quickly as I can.

When we get home, I help Mami clean and then we take the sheets and towels and clothes to wash and dry in the machines in the basement. It's dark and creepy down there, like a dungeon. We're both a little afraid as we sit and wait on a bench in front of the machines. Mami says we can't go upstairs and come back when it's all done because our things might get stolen.

"Why would anyone want to steal our old stuff?" I ask.

Mami replies, "There are people even more poor than us."

It's four o'clock in the afternoon when we finish.

"Now can I go out and play, Mami?"

"Just for a little while. Papi will be home soon. You know he gets home early on Saturdays."

I run down with my chalk and draw a long hopscotch board, adding flowers to the corners again. No one else is outside, so I play a few rounds by myself.

Danielle must see me from her window across the street, and Ava and June must just have a feeling I'm outside, because a few minutes later the three of them show up.

We play a few rounds and I win them all.

Danielle is wearing her black go-go boots again.

"Guess what?" I announce proudly. "My father just got me go-go boots too!"

"So why aren't you wearing them?" Danielle replies.

Ava says, "Yeah, why not?"

June chimes in, "If I had go-go boots, I'd never take them off."

"I don't want them to get dirty."

Ava and June burst out laughing. Ava says, "But remember what the song says?" She sings, "'These boots are made for walkin','" and June joins in, "'And that's just what they'll do.'"

"Shut your mouths!" I yell. "You think I don't know the song? The boots cost a lot of money. I have to take care of them."

Danielle nods her head as if she understands. "Ruthie, will you wear the boots to school on Monday? We can both wear our boots! Won't that be fun?"

"Sure!" I tell her, hoping my mother will let me wear them to school.

"Très magnifique!" Danielle says in her high-pitched voice.

We play another round of hopscotch. But I've decided Ava and June are not really my friends. Only Danielle is my friend.

It's my turn and I am about to throw my stone down on the hopscotch board, but then I look up and see a sky-blue car with long white fins pull up to the curb. A man with dark hair and a dark mustache steps out and walks toward me . . . Wait, it's Papi! But how can it be Papi?

"Papi, whose car is that?"

"It's ours, Ruti! I just bought it."

"Wow, Papi, that's great!"

"It's an Oldsmobile. The car I used to dream about in Cuba."

I give Papi a kiss and a hug, the way he likes. Danielle, Ava, and June stare at us. Maybe they're jealous. No one has such a fancy car in our neighborhood.

"Can we go for a ride? Please, Papi!"

"Later," Papi says. "Let's go surprise your mother first."

"Mami will be happy we have a car! Now we can go anyplace we want!"

"I hope she'll be happy." Papi sighs. "I never know with your mother." He takes my hand. *"Bueno, vamos."*

"Bye, Danielle. Bye, Ava. Bye, June. See you later!"

The moment the elevator opens on the sixth floor, I rush out and ring the doorbell, excited to tell Mami the news. But Mami doesn't come to the door right away, so Papi lets us in with his key.

"Mami? Mami? Where are you?"

Mami is still at the window, where she often sits, watching the world go by. Now there's worry in her voice as she says, "Don't tell me, Alberto. You didn't buy that car, did you?"

Papi smiles from ear to ear like a little boy. "I did! It's such a beauty and I always wanted a blue Oldsmobile when we lived in Cuba. Now we're in America and I have one."

"Ay, Alberto, but we don't have money for a car."

Papi smooths his curly hair with his hands and tries not

to raise his voice. "I took out a loan. Stop worrying. We'll pay it back *poco a poco.*"

Poco a poco. Little by little—that's one of Papi's favorite expressions.

"We don't need a car," Mami moans. "Let's wait a year or two."

Papi makes a fist with his right hand and punches his left palm. And he shouts, "I'm breaking my back taking the subway every day! Working all week in a dingy office that has no windows and is the size of a jail cell where they treat me like I'm nobody! On top of that I spend Saturday fumigating apartments. Everything I do is to support you and the children. So don't *you* tell me I can't have a car!"

"I'm sorry, Alberto," Mami whispers back.

I feel scared for Mami. She's wearing the flip-flops she uses only in the house when she's very tired. Without her heels, she looks smaller than small. I take hold of her hand, not much bigger than mine. We sink into a corner of the Castro convertible sofa.

Papi turns his back on us and walks away. He goes into the bathroom and slams the door. Mami tightens her grip on my hand. Will he remain angry for hours? We hear Papi turn on the shower. We wait, holding our breaths. After a few minutes, he starts humming tunes in Spanish.

"*Cha-cha-cha, qué rico cha-cha-cha.*"

Mami and I smile at each other, relieved.

"*Ay, qué bueno,*" she says.

Papi returns to the living room in the fresh clothes Mami set out for him. He smells like he spilled the whole bottle of

Old Spice on his cheeks. He smiles at Mami, sits down, and takes her other hand. In a gentle voice, he says, "Rebequita, don't worry, we'll manage. Have a little faith in me. I'll take a third job if we need more money. It was my big dream to have a car. I couldn't have it in Cuba, but I can have it in America. You don't want to rob me of that. Rob me of my dream?"

"Alberto, I want you to be happy."

"I want you to be happy too, Rebequita. Let's try to be happy, *mi amor*."

Papi takes Mami into his arms. They kiss and hug. But even as he's holding Mami tight, Papi doesn't let go of the car keys in his right hand.

We hear the doorbell ringing, ringing, ringing. Izzie rushes in, red-faced, sweaty, in muddy clothes.

"Papi, all the kids say so, but I don't believe them. Is that Oldsmobile really ours?"

Smiling, Papi replies, "*Sí, niño*, it's our car."

"When can we go for a ride, Papi? Please, Papi, can we go now?"

Izzie dances in circles around Papi like a wind-up toy.

Finally Papi says, "I've had a long day at work. But tomorrow we go for a ride. You'll see, children, this is the land of opportunity and *poco a poco* all our dreams will come true. Now I have to rest. Who's going to get me my slippers?"

Papi's blue Oldsmobile

On Sunday, Mami and Papi sleep late. They stay tucked under the sheets on the Castro convertible, in no rush to do anything, giggling with each other. Even after she gets up and takes a shower, Mami doesn't rush to fold up the bed and turn it back into a sofa.

While Papi sings his cha-cha-cha song in the shower, Mami asks me to translate the pancake recipe that's printed on the Aunt Jemima box. She lets me break the eggs into the mix and we make a nice stack of pancakes. I tell Mami we're supposed to have the pancakes with maple syrup, but we don't have maple syrup, so we sprinkle sugar on them and they taste good.

After I help Mami clean up all the breakfast dishes, she gives me a hug and says, "*Gracias*, Ruti."

Then it's time to get ready for our first big trip in our sky-blue Oldsmobile. We're going to Staten Island! Gladys and Oscar, who are Mami and Papi's friends from Cuba, live there and they have a baby girl named Rosa. Papi says it will be a breeze to get to Staten Island in our car. Otherwise, we'd have to take two subways from Queens to Manhattan and then the ferry.

I wait with Papi and Izzie in the living room. The bed is a sofa again. The three of us sit there while Mami styles her hair and puts on her makeup in the bathroom.

After a while, Papi grows impatient. He yells, *"¡Vamos! ¡Rápido!"*

"¡Un momento!" Mami yells back.

Finally Mami appears. She looks like a movie star! She's wearing a yellow dress with a matching yellow jacket. Her beige high heels match her beige purse. She has round black sunglasses and a thin scarf tied at her neck to keep her hair tidy.

We pile into the Oldsmobile. Mami sits in the front with Papi. I sit in the back with Izzie. And we have to make room for Baba. We try to get Zeide to come, but he wants to stay home. "I'm tired from working six days a week at Super Discount Fabric. I need to rest," he says.

Zeide and Baba had a fabric store in Cuba, but Fidel Castro took it away when he decided everything should be owned by the government. They miss their store in Cuba. It was small but it was theirs. Now they both work at Super Discount Fabric on Roosevelt Avenue, a street crowded with immigrants like us looking for cheap things. Baba is so busy she wears her scissors on a chain around her neck to always have them ready. She complains about the headaches she gets working there. The store is under the Number 7 train and rattles like a maraca.

Baba loves our new car. "It rides so smoothly," she says. "I feel like I'm floating in the ocean." She squeezes my hand with both of hers, which are rough from cutting calico and canvas all day.

Papi drives very slowly on the highway. The other cars whip past us. He laughs as they go by. "Let them go as fast as they want. They don't bother me and I don't bother them. This is America, a free country, no?"

Next to me, Izzie plays with his toy Cadillac. "Zoom, zoom, zoom," he says, as his feet press against the back of Papi's seat.

"Stop it, Izzie!" Papi shouts.

Izzie settles down and whispers in my ear, "It's dumb to drive for an hour just to see a baby sleeping in a crib."

"Babies are cute," I tell him. "And cuddly."

"No, they're not. They cry a lot. And poop their pants."

But baby Rosa is smiling when we arrive. She's only six months old and already can sit up. She has tiny gold balls in her pierced ears and a gold bracelet that says "Rosa" wrapped around her pudgy wrist. Her eyes are two dark moons and when she stares at you she looks like she can see through you.

Gladys says if I sit very still on the sofa, she'll let me hold baby Rosa. In my arms she feels fuzzy and soft and smells like the pancakes that Mami and I made for breakfast. Even Izzie thinks she's sweet and he makes funny faces to make Rosa smile.

Mami glances around at the gleaming wood furniture and at the ceiling lamp that has big teardrop crystals dangling from it. She looks down at the white shag wool rug and tells Gladys, *"Tienes una casa muy bonita."* A very pretty house.

"We're happy here. Oscar got a good job in engineering, which he loves, and he's earning more than he did in Cuba," Gladys replies, stroking the gleaming diamond ring on her finger. "Of course you're welcome to visit us anytime." She smiles and pats Mami's hand. *"Mi casa es su casa."*

"If only we lived a little closer." Mami sighs.

"I know, Rebequita," Gladys moans. "In Havana, if I needed a cup of sugar, all I had to do was knock on your door."

"At least we have a car now. But I can't drive. I doubt I ever will. The highways here make me nervous. I'll always have to depend on Alberto."

"Ladies, let's not be sad. What can I offer you to drink?" Oscar says, throwing an arm around Papi's shoulder. "What do you say we have a drink and celebrate our being together again?"

Oscar fills the glasses with rum and Coca-Cola and passes them to Mami and Papi and Gladys. "And you too, Señora Ester?" he asks Baba, winking at her. "Or do you prefer just the Coca-Cola?"

"I'm not a little girl anymore and I'm not an old lady yet," Baba replies.

Oscar claps his hands, fills her glass, and says, *"¡Qué bueno!* That's the spirit! Let's toast to a free Cuba! *¡Una Cuba libre!"*

He turns to Izzie and me. "And for you, *niños*, how about apple juice?"

We're both disappointed. Izzie asks, "Mami, could we have Coca-Cola?"

She shakes her head. "No, you can't. You'll both get so wild you'll be doing the mambo."

"Give them each a Coca-Cola," Papi orders. "It's a special occasion and one soda won't do them any harm."

"*Gracias*, Papi," Izzie says.

Papi nods with a stern gaze. "But behave. Don't spill it."

I pass baby Rosa back to Gladys and get comfortable on the sofa. I sip from the tall glass of Coca-Cola, crossing my legs to show off my go-go boots, wishing we lived in such a nice house.

"What pretty boots you have, Ruti!" Gladys says.

"*Muchas gracias,*" I respond politely.

Mami starts laughing. "She likes those boots so much she wants to wear them to sleep. Can you imagine?"

"Well, they're very stylish," Gladys says. "Isn't there a song they're singing now about boots? I heard it on the radio the other day."

"I know it by heart! Is it okay if I sing?" I ask.

"Of course, *mi niña*. Sing it for us," Gladys replies.

I stand up and sing at the top of my lungs:

> *These boots are made for walkin'*
> *And that's just what they'll do . . .*

I do my imitation of the dance routine from TV and finish with the finale:

Are you ready, boots?
Start walkin'!

Everyone claps, even poor Izzie, who's jealous and was pretending to be playing with his toy Cadillac the whole time I was singing.

I sit back down next to baby Rosa, who has started to fidget in her mother's arms. I notice a smell that's not so nice.

"Did baby Rosa just poop?" I ask.

"Ruti, what a sharp nose you have," Gladys says. "You noticed before I did that it's time to change her diaper."

After baby Rosa gets a fresh diaper, she falls asleep and Gladys takes Mami, Baba, and me to her room so we can see how pretty it is. Flying birds are painted on the walls and her crib is white, her canopy is white, and her blanket is white with ruffles along the edges. It's a bedroom fit for a baby girl who'll grow up to be a princess.

Gladys serves dinner in the dining room. We sit on chairs with red velvet seats and eat meat loaf with an egg cooked into the middle, chicken croquettes, black beans and white rice, fried plantains, and a salad with avocados. For dessert we each get a bowl of grated coconut in really thick syrup.

"*Delicioso,*" Mami and Papi say.

Oscar turns to Papi. "I have a couple of cigars left, from Cuba. Want one, Alberto?"

"*Sí, claro,*" Papi says, beaming.

While the grown-ups sit at the table, telling jokes and

laughing, I go back to the baby's room to spy on Rosa, listening to her breathe and let out little sighs as she dreams.

When I return to the living room, it's dark outside but no one is in a rush.

"Remember how we sat on the balcony at night listening to the palm trees sway in the breeze?" Gladys says.

Mami replies, "How can I forget? Oh, Cuba, our beloved Cuba."

"We can't keep looking back," Baba whispers.

"It's all gone now, anyway," Papi says, still puffing on his cigar.

Oscar puffs on his cigar too. "The important thing is we're here and we'll always be friends." He notices Izzie and me sitting there quietly. "You've both behaved very well. Here's some M&M's for you!" And he gives us each a packet. Yippee!

Izzie and I tear into the M&M's and finish them in no time. No one scolds us; no one seems to mind.

Then our visit starts coming to an end, our special day about to be over.

"¡Vamos!" Papi orders. "Tomorrow is Monday. We all have to get up early."

Tomorrow Izzie and I will be in school. It will be my first day in the smart class!

We make our way slowly to the door.

"Bye, Gladys! Bye, Oscar. ¡Gracias!"

"Come back and see us again soon," Gladys calls out.

"We will," Mami says, waving happily and throwing her old friend a kiss.

I feel so happy and grown-up wearing my go-go boots.

I bring my lips to the palm of my hand, blowing my kiss into the night air of Staten Island, hoping the wind will carry it across the hills and plains of the vast land of America that gave Papi the blue Oldsmobile of his dreams.

lucky

I lean against Baba's shoulder in the backseat of the car and she says, "Lie down, be comfortable, *shayna maideleh*." I feel loved like baby Rosa when I sink into her lap and she uses those sugar words that mean "beautiful girl" in Yiddish.

I curl my legs under me so as not to crowd Izzie and peer up at the roof of the car. The reflections of the headlights and taillights move in different directions. I am lulled to sleep by the swooshing sound of the car sailing down the highway, the ride so smooth, like Baba said. I'm floating along on a calm ocean. Words drift past me, Baba and Mami talking about baby Rosa.

Then everything goes still. There's no swoosh. There are no voices. I open my eyes. My head isn't on Baba's lap anymore. Baba is gone. Izzie is gone. Mami and Papi are gone. I am all by myself in the car.

Where am I?

Where is everyone?

I try to get up, but I'm only wearing one go-go boot. I've lost the boot on my left leg. And my right leg is twisted weirdly. I can't move it. I don't think it's my leg. It's someone else's leg.

Am I dreaming?

I close my eyes and try to go back to sleep. But I can't sleep because my leg hurts like nothing ever hurt before.

Out of the darkness a man appears. He looks in through the broken windows, struggles with the lock on the back door, and finally flings it open.

Who is this man? Blood is dripping from the top of his head.

It's Papi!

"Papi! Papi! Why did you all leave me? Papi, I lost one of my boots. Can we go look for it?"

"Later. The car might catch fire."

He bends and picks me up, trying to cradle my right leg in the crook of his arm. But the leg flops down like the legs of my old rag doll from Cuba.

"Stop, Papi! It hurts!"

"Calma, calma."

Papi keeps walking and when we get to the edge of the highway he lays me down on the ground. Mami is there with Baba. They are holding hands and crying like little girls. Papi looks up at the sky and shouts, *"¡Dios mío!* Why? Why? Why?"

Izzie's head is bleeding like Papi's, but he's not in any pain. Izzie thinks we're having an adventure. He kneels next to me and says, "I saw it! I saw a car flip the divider! It turned into a torpedo! I saw it crash into the car in front of us! Then we crashed into them. Then a bunch of cars

41

crashed into us! Bam, bam, bam." Izzie waits for me to say something. I'm quiet, so he continues, "It was like a movie!"

It's stupid but I feel jealous of Izzie. Why did I have to fall asleep?

From somewhere in the darkness, beyond where I can see, a woman moans.

"Oh, oh, oh, oh . . ."

The night is black and blue and purple like an ugly bruise.

Who will help us? Who will take us home?

In the distance, I hear a siren. The wail grows louder and louder as the ambulance comes closer. Finally the ambulance stops right next to us.

Two men jump out and take a quick look at all of us.

"*Aquí, aquí,*" I hear Papi say. "*Mi hija,*" he stammers.

The woman moans again. "Oh, oh, oh, oh . . ."

The men rush over to where the woman is.

"She's breathing," one man says. "But she's tangled up in metal. This is going to take a while. Put a splint on that girl. Take her and her family to the hospital. See if any of them can speak English."

I want to shout, "I speak English!" But I've forgotten how to talk.

The man who is supposed to attend to me says, "We need another ambulance. And we need a funeral car. Why aren't the cops here by now? There's a bunch of dead people."

Dead people?

He comes over to me and bends down to look at my leg. He smells like a White Castle hamburger with shiny onions on top.

"Listen, kid. Try not to move, okay? You understand?"

He brings out a slab of wood from the ambulance. Then he lifts my leg and uses thick tape to strap it down.

It hurts like crazy. I can't hold back the tears.

"Come on, kid, be brave."

He brings out a stretcher and sets me down on it.

"Are you all right? Can you help?" he asks Papi.

"Yes, sir. This is nothing," Papi says and he points to his bloody head.

He and Papi carry me to the ambulance. The man tells Papi to sit with him in the front. Mami and Baba follow us with Izzie. They cram in around me in the back of the ambulance.

Now Izzie is exhausted. He says to Mami, "Are we going home?"

That only makes her cry all over again.

The siren blares as the man takes us away in the ambulance.

The darkness of the night creeps into my heart. I think about how Papi should have listened to Mami and not bought the blue Oldsmobile.

I want to yell, "It's your fault, Papi, all your fault!"

But I just lie there and listen to Mami repeat over and over, "Why didn't we stay in Cuba? Why didn't we stay in Cuba? Why didn't we stay in Cuba?"

At the hospital, people moan and cry. There are so many of them, everyone lined up on stretchers, one after another. No one pays any attention to their moans or their cries.

I lie on a stretcher moaning and crying too.

Mami and Baba and Izzie and Papi stand around me like

43

bowling pins about to topple over. There's no place for them to sit.

A nurse comes over in her squeaky nurse shoes.

"You can't all be here in the emergency room. It's too crowded. Go to the waiting room. I'll keep you informed of the girl's progress."

They're half asleep and don't move right away.

The nurse raises her voice. "Don't you people understand English?"

She shoos them out the door like pesky flies.

I am left alone with all the miserable people.

Then there's a big commotion.

"Out of the way! Out of the way! This is urgent!"

They wheel in a woman on a stretcher, her arms and legs limp, her eyes open too wide.

A doctor in a white coat runs toward her and bumps into my stretcher.

"It hurts, it hurts," I stammer as loud as I can to get his attention.

"Quiet, kid," he says to me. "You've just got a broken leg. You're lucky. This woman here, she was in the car in front of you. She'll probably never walk again. We think she is paralyzed for life."

Another doctor in a white coat finally comes and gives me an injection and I fall asleep. When I wake up, I don't know what day it is. I'm in a hospital bed and my right leg hangs from a strap tied to the ceiling.

A nurse comes in. She snips off my underwear with a huge pair of scissors and throws the pieces in the trash. She leaves me wearing only a hospital gown.

"Where are my go-go boots?"

"Gone," the nurse replies. "You can't wear them anyway."

"What do I do if I have to go to the bathroom?"

"Call me when you need the bedpan," she says. "Press the button before you have to go, not after you wet the bed. I only change the sheets once a day."

"Where are my mami and papi?" I ask her.

"They had to go," she says. "Now try to sleep."

After she leaves, I stare at the clock, trying to make the time go faster. I can't believe I have been abandoned, left all alone in the world. I keep repeating words to myself until they become a song in my head:

> *No one loves me*
> *not even my mother*
> *not even my father*
> *not even my brother*
> Nadie me quiere a mí . . .

I've given up on ever seeing my family again when Mami bursts through the door with Aunt Sylvia and Uncle Bill. I want to run over and give them hugs but I can't move.

Mami comes to my bed and smooths my messy ponytails with her hands. *"Mi niña, mi niña,"* she says in her sad voice that is sadder than ever.

"Here, sit down, Rebeca," says Uncle Bill and brings her a chair from the other side of the room.

As she arranges herself on the chair, I notice Mami has cuts and scratches all over her arms and legs.

"Mami, are you okay?"

"*No es nada.* That's just from the broken glass of the car windows. Don't worry about me, *mi niña.* It's you I'm worried about."

"What about Papi? And Izzie?"

"Papi and Izzie got a few stitches on their heads, but they're fine. Papi went back to work and he made Izzie return to school."

"And Baba?"

"Baba is at home. She couldn't sleep last night. She's afraid another catastrophe will happen. The doctor gave her pills to calm her nerves."

"Poor Baba."

"Don't worry, *mi niña.* Please don't worry."

Uncle Bill comes up to my bed. "So I hear you broke a leg," he says. "Or are you pretending? How about if I untie you from this contraption and take you home?" He reaches for the strap and acts like he's pulling on it.

"No, Uncle Bill, don't!"

He laughs. "Fooled you, didn't I?"

Uncle Bill pulls a rolled-up newspaper out of his back pocket.

"Look, you made the front page of the *Daily News.* Your names are here."

Uncle Bill shows me Papi's name (Mr. Alberto Mizrahi)

46

and Mami's name (Mrs. Rebecca Mizrahi) and my name (Ruth) and my brother's name (Isaac) and Baba's name (Mrs. Esther Glinienski). He reads aloud, "All were taken to Brookdale Hospital, where only Ruth was detained for a fractured right leg."

He smiles. "So what do you think? You're famous!"

"Yeah, I'm famous," I say. "Famous for my stupid broken leg."

Mami gets upset. "*Mi niña*, don't let me hear you say the word 'stupid' to your uncle Bill. That's not nice."

There's a sharp knock on the door. A very tall man enters. He has bushy eyebrows and big eyeglasses. "Hello, I'm Dr. Friendlich," he says.

Mami and Aunt Sylvia lower their heads. Not Uncle Bill. He looks the doctor in the eye. "How long are you keeping my niece in the hospital?"

Dr. Friendlich replies curtly, "As long as necessary."

He taps my leg. I wince and he says to me, "Hurts, doesn't it?" Then he turns back to Uncle Bill. "She needs surgery. Bad break to the femur."

Uncle Bill shrugs. "Kids break bones all the time. You'll fix her up like new, won't you?"

"I hope so. But in medicine, there are no guarantees, I am sorry to say."

Dr. Friendlich turns away from Uncle Bill and sniffs around my bed.

I realize there is a big wet circle under me.

Dr. Friendlich smiles and pats my hand. "A little accident, huh, young lady? We'll get that taken care of right away." He pokes his head out the door. "Nurse! Come change the sheets."

The nurse gives me a nasty look as she enters the room.

She tells Dr. Friendlich, "I told her to call me before she needed to go."

"Give the child another chance. She's new to this. She'll do better tomorrow." Then Dr. Friendlich looks at us, nods, and says, "Good-bye for now."

The nurse commands Mami, Sylvia, and Bill, "Wait outside."

The nurse lectures me as she pulls off the wet sheets. "Learn to control yourself, missy. I don't have time to be changing your sheets all day. Next time you have an accident I'll let you lie in it and you'll see what's good for you."

I can't believe that this is all happening. Yesterday I was a normal girl. I went to the bathroom by myself. Today I can't do anything without the help of a mean nurse.

Resting again on nice clean sheets, I ask her, "Nurse, do you hate me especially? Or do you just hate all kids?"

The nurse stares at me in shock. I wonder what awful thing she will say.

She is quiet for a minute and then she says, "I don't hate you, missy. I don't hate all children. I guess I'm just angry at the world. You see, I have a daughter at home who's been sick since she was born. All I want is to be with my girl and take care of her. But I have to work to support us, and my mother too. Every day I leave my girl with her grandma, who can barely take care of herself, and hope they'll be okay until I get home. So I'm angry. Understand?"

Something happens to my heart; it cracks like the sugar crust on Mami's flan, hearing the nurse talk to me that way.

"I understand, Nurse. I'm really sorry."

"Don't be sorry. It's not your fault. I've been mean to you and that wasn't right. How about if I bring you an ice cream sandwich? Would you like that?"

"Thank you!"

"Okay. And please remember to ring the bell if you need the bedpan."

"I will, Nurse. I promise."

"Please call me by my name. It's Neala. It's an Irish name. But my family's been here such a long time we don't remember a thing about dear old Ireland."

Poor Neala, who forgot the land where she was born. I wonder if a day will come when I will forget Cuba. I hope not. But it already seems far, far away, and as hard to hold on to as sea spray.

The next morning, Nurse Neala brings in the bedpan and taps my shoulder to wake me up.

"Sorry to rush you, dear, but you need to empty your bladder now, before they take you in for surgery."

After Neala leaves, two men in green uniforms arrive and wheel me into the operating room. Dr. Friendlich is there, waiting for me.

"Hello, Ruthie," Dr. Friendlich says. "We're going to give you anesthesia and you won't feel a thing."

"But I don't like shots!" I wail.

"Just close your eyes. It will be over before you know it."

When I wake up, I feel funny. I don't know if the person who has woken is still me. I'm now crammed inside something.

What is it?

A box?

Why can't I get out?

Is it a coffin? Am I dead?

I can't be dead. I see Mami wiping tears from her eyes and Papi is pacing back and forth.

I want to cheer them up. "Hi, Mami. Hi, Papi. I'm okay. Let's go home!"

Mami lays a moist palm on my forehead. "Oh, my little girl!"

Dr. Friendlich knocks on the door and barges in, followed by Neala. He comes straight to my bed and pulls away the sheet that's spread over me.

"Stop!" I scream. "No!"

I'm afraid there will be nothing to cover my private parts. I place my hands there, one over the other, to cover myself. But what is this dress I'm wearing? What is this heavy white garment that won't let me move?

"¡Silencio!" Papi says. "Never yell at the doctor, mi hija."

Papi lifts his chin to gaze up at Dr. Friendlich. "Doctor?"

Dr. Friendlich is so tall he's used to looking down at everyone. "Yes?"

I can tell Papi is struggling to find the right words. He's sweating and wiping his forehead with a white handkerchief that Mami has starched and ironed for him.

50

"Why did you make my daughter into a mummy?"

"I'm sorry, Mr. Mizrahi," Dr. Friendlich says. "We had to put your daughter in a body cast. She's growing. We want to prevent one leg from ending up shorter than the other. We hope it will work."

A body cast . . . So that's why both legs are locked away and my tummy and hips are also locked away. The plaster reaches to my chest and around my back.

I'm a mummy but I'm not dead.

"Get her a pillow, Nurse," Dr. Friendlich says.

Neala lifts my head and tucks the pillow under my neck.

Now I can see my toes. They stick out of the cast, my ten toes. I can't wiggle them. I can't move anything except for my head, my shoulders, and my arms. And I have an opening in front and another in back for me to be able to pee and poop. My legs are spread apart and there's a pole between them like the letter A.

Dr. Friendlich turns to Mami. "The nurse will show you how to use the pole. You'll be able to turn your daughter on her stomach, so she can sleep. You'll need to wash her without getting the cast wet. The nurse will show you how to lift her, so she can use the bedpan. Other than that, do not move her."

Mami nods and pretends to understand. I listen carefully. I'll have to explain it all to her later in Spanish.

"How long she will be a mummy?" Papi asks.

"We don't know," Dr. Friendlich replies. "Probably about six months . . ."

Papi's forehead is creased with worry lines. "My daughter . . . she will walk? Or she will not walk?"

51

Dr. Friendlich pats me on the head. "You want to walk, Ruthie, don't you?"

"Yes, Doctor," I whisper.

"Then you will walk," Dr. Friendlich says. He pats my head again.

To Papi he says, "Give it time."

Dr. Friendlich spreads the sheet over me. I look through his large glasses and into his eyes. He's gazing at me with kindness and also with sadness.

"Young lady, pray to God and all the saints and your guardian angels."

That night I lie in my hospital bed, all alone, without my mother, without my father, without my brother, without my family, without a friend. I do as the doctor says and I make up a prayer.

Dear God,

I came from Cuba to start a new life in the United States of America.

I begged for go-go boots and got them.

I shouldn't have asked for them. I was showing off too much.

I shouldn't have been so proud to be Miss Hopscotch Queen of Queens.

I must have done a lot of bad things to end up like this, in a body cast.

My leg is fractured, but all of me broke. Who'll put me together again?

And I know I'm lucky. I'm not as broken as some other people.

I promise to be good for the rest of my life if you listen to my prayer and make me well again.

I promise I will commiserate with broken people all over the whole wide world from now on and forever.

Thank you,

Ruthie

PART II

MY BED
IS
MY ISLAND

a baby in diapers again

After a week in the hospital, Dr. Friendlich says I'm ready to go home. Early in the morning, Mami and Papi come to pick me up. Two men named Bobbie and Clay strap me to a stretcher and take me outside.

I am so happy to see the sun again, and the clouds in the sky like shag wool rugs, and people who aren't sick.

"Is that a bird singing?" I say.

"Yes, child, it took a while, but spring has finally decided to grace us with its presence," Clay replies. He has a kind and lilting voice.

"You don't talk like they do in New York. Where are you from?"

"I'm from down south, from Mississippi, where they say the livin' is easy, but not so much for a man with black skin. I came to New York and I'm never goin' back."

Clay smiles and pats my head. Now everyone pats my head. Then he slides me into the back of the ambulance as if shutting a drawer.

Bobbie says, "What do you think, Ruthie? We'll turn on

the siren real loud and watch everyone scoot out of our way. Won't that be lots of fun?" Bobbie has red hair that glows in the sun like a lightbulb.

"Yeah, lots of fun," I reply, to be polite, even though I am frightened by the siren's mournful wail.

Papi sits in front with the men. Mami is crouched on the rickety bench next to me. Off we go, the ambulance racing past yellow and red lights.

Mami clutches the window handle. "*Ay, Dios mío,* what if we get into another car accident?"

I try to be funny. "Nothing to worry about, Mami! We're already in an ambulance."

"Poo, poo," Mami says. "Don't joke."

The ambulance stops, and the wailing siren clicks off. Clay pulls open the door and gives Mami a hand getting down. Then Bobbie comes around, and between him and Clay they slide me out of the ambulance and carry me on the stretcher.

Aunt Sylvia and Uncle Bill are waiting outside. Izzie and Dennis and Lily come running with all the kids from the neighborhood. Bobbie and Clay were right—returning home in an ambulance, with the siren on, is fun.

Except that Danielle is standing on the hopscotch board in her go-go boots. Why doesn't she come over and say something?

Ava and June and the other kids all crowd around. "Ruthie, Ruthie."

They demand, "Show us your cast. Come on, let's see

your cast." And they draw closer to me until I can smell their sweat from playing hard in the sun. I feel nervous. I don't want to be here. But I'm unable to move or run away.

"Later, okay?" I tell them. "I'll let you all sign it then."

"We want to see it now! Now! Now! Now!"

Lily comes and tugs on the blanket, like it's a game.

"Stop it!" I scream. "No!"

I only have on an undershirt and a blouse. Below the blouse I'm covered by a sheet and a blanket. I can't wear underwear. It doesn't fit over the cast. I will die of embarrassment if they see me naked.

Fortunately Bobbie waves his hands, shooing the kids away. "We have to get Ruthie home. Get her settled. Kids, how about you run and play? Another day you'll visit Ruthie."

The kids wait, watching. They are all curious.

In his booming voice, Uncle Bill shouts, "You heard what he said. Get going. Come on. Scram."

Finally the kids scurry off, except for Izzie.

"You can stay. You're her brother," Uncle Bill says. "But don't act wild."

"Okay," Izzie says. He steps next to the stretcher, looking at me as if I were not his sister but some kind of strange bug.

Papi leads the way to the entrance of the building. Aunt Sylvia puts an arm around Mami. Uncle Bill takes Izzie's hand.

We don't all fit in the elevator. Clay, Bobbie, me, Mami, and Sylvia squeeze in tight.

"We'll race you!" Izzie says.

Izzie, Papi, and Uncle Bill take the stairs up to the sixth floor. When the elevator opens on our floor, Izzie is already there, panting.

Clay and Bobbie cross through the dining room into the living room and take me down the hall to the bedroom. They whisk me off the stretcher and lift me down slowly into my bed. After white sheets at the hospital, I am glad to see my colorful sheets decorated with yellow and orange marigolds.

"Darlin,' you take it easy now, you hear?" Clay says.

Bobbie adds, "Bye, kid."

"But wait! Who will move me from place to place once you two are gone?"

Bobbie looks back at me and shakes his head. "The doctor says you're not to be moved for a while. Your parents can turn you on your stomach with the pole, but that's it. You need to lie still. We'll be back when it's time to change your cast. See you then. Bye now!"

As Clay and Bobbie go out the door, Izzie comes running in with a package of Chips Ahoy!

"Hey, Roofie, you want a chocolate chip cookie?"

Mami snatches the package from him. "Only one cookie a week for your sister! She can't gain weight or she won't fit into the cast."

"It's okay, I don't want any. I'm not hungry," I say. "But I gotta pee."

"How are you gonna pee?" Izzie asks.

"Just get out of the room!" I yell. "Don't you dare come

60

back till I say the coast is clear!"

"Why are you screaming at your brother?" Mami says. "He's a little boy. He doesn't know."

She leaves and comes back with the shiny new bedpan and a roll of toilet paper. She lifts me with the pole, the way the nurse showed her, and slides the bedpan under my backside. The bedpan is ice-cold. It's made of steel.

I pee a lot.

"Okay, I'm done!" I yell and Mami comes running back.

I dry myself with toilet paper, roll the wet toilet paper in some unused toilet paper, and hand it to Mami. She lifts me and grabs the bedpan, trying not to spill the pee all over the bed.

From now on, every time I need to pee, Mami will have to help me.

When I poop too.

Just the other day I felt so grown-up in my go-go boots. And now I'm like a baby in diapers again.

get well

In the morning Mrs. Sarota pays me a visit. It's the first time a teacher has ever come to our house. She brings a "get well" card signed by the kids in my old class. Their messages have lots of spelling mistakes, but they are so sweet.

> Sory you brock your leg, Roothie. Must hert reely bad.

> I feel terible you canot go out to the park and play like a regula kid.

> Hope u get well reeeeel fassssst.

Mami lifts the sheets on either side of me so Mrs. Sarota can see the cast. I don't worry anymore about people seeing me naked. Now I keep a towel over my private parts, that way I am always covered.

Mrs. Sarota looks like she's going to have a heart attack when she sees my body in the cast, the plaster reaching all the way to my chest so I can't even sit up.

"I'm going to inform the school right away," she says in a serious voice. "This is terrible. Just terrible."

I don't think Mrs. Sarota realizes that she's making me feel like I'm a rotten person for making her feel so bad.

She asks Mami, "How long will Ruth need to be in the cast?"

Mami glances at me to be sure she understands the question. After I translate it into Spanish, she says, "A long time. The doctor's *muy* sorry, *muy* sad."

"This is such a pity," Mrs. Sarota replies. "And I just promoted Ruth."

Why is Mrs. Sarota talking like I'm not there?

"I'm not going to have to go back to the dumb class, am I?" I ask.

Mrs. Sarota pats my head. Why does everyone pat my head?

"You poor dear," Mrs. Sarota replies. "I'm going to do everything in my power to help you."

That afternoon, Ramu slips a letter under the door.

After Mami brings it to me, I just hold it for a while and enjoy its aroma. It smells warm and spicy, and also sweet from the sandalwood incense that Ramu's mother burns in their apartment to keep the spirits happy.

Ramu writes:

Dear Ruthie,

I hope you get well soon. I am sad you got hurt and didn't get to join the smart class with me. It is lonely there by myself, not knowing anyone.

I am sorry I can't visit you. My mother still doesn't want Avik and me to play with kids who aren't Indian like us.

I miss you. I promise one day I will sneak out and come see you.

Your friend,
Ramu

P.S. Avik says he also misses you.

I ask Mami for a pen and paper and I write a letter back to Ramu, even though it takes a long time. I have to hold the pad up in the air with one arm and try to carefully write the words down so they don't come out too sloppy. It's hard to write when you're flat on your back and squeezed into a body cast!

Dear Ramu,

Everyone says get well and that is nice, but it will be months and months before I get well. I have to lie in bed and wait. And hope. Even the doctor says there are no guarantees. He told me to pray to God and all the saints. I never used to pray but now I do say little prayers.

I wish you didn't feel lonely in the smart class. Pretend

I'm sitting next to you and we are reading "The Princess Who Could Not Cry" like we used to.

I miss you too. And I miss Avik.

Tell your mother I know about guavas and mangos. That makes me a little bit Indian, don't you think?

Your friend,

Ruthie

P.S. I'm going to ask Izzie to place this letter in your hands, so you don't get in trouble.

When Izzie comes home from playing, Mami orders him to wash up and change his clothes before she'll let him have his chocolate milk.

I hear them yelling at each other in the living room.

"Mami, I'm thirsty! Let me have a sip!"

"No, *mi niño*. Do as I say, *por favor*. Or do you want me to tell Papi when he gets home?"

Izzie storms into the room. "Hi, Roofie," he says. "Mami is being very mean today."

"She's just tired, Izzie. But you be a good boy, okay?"

"Okay, thanks, Roofie," he says and reaches over and hugs me. He smells like the street—like the grass I can't step on.

Izzie throws open a drawer and pulls out clean pants and a clean shirt. I turn my head as he slips out of the old clothes into the new. We've always shared a room, so we're used to looking away when one of us is changing.

He's about to rush out of the room, then turns back and asks, "Hey, Roofie, you want some chocolate milk?"

"I can't have any. Mami says I'll burst out of the cast," I tell him, trying to act like it's funny.

But Izzie realizes it's not funny. "Sorry, Roofie," he says. "You can't have cookies, you can't have chocolate milk. What can you have that's good?"

"Maybe you could get me a glass of water?"

"Sure."

He runs off on legs that he knows will take him where he wants to go. I've already forgotten what that feels like.

A minute later he runs back with the water for me.

"Here, Roofie."

Izzie watches as I sip the water slowly so I don't spill it. I dip my face down, as if I had a beak and were a sparrow drinking from a fountain.

"It's gonna take you till tomorrow to finish that water," he says.

"That's okay. I'm not going anywhere," I say.

"Roofie, that's not funny."

"Well, in the hospital they had straws. That made it easier."

Izzie shakes his head and looks sad. He runs out and I hear him say to Mami, "We don't have any? Not even one?"

Mami says, "Go ask Aunt Sylvia. Maybe she'll have some."

The front door slams as Izzie rushes out. I imagine him racing down the stairs to the fourth floor.

Minutes later he's back.

"Look what I got you, Roofie."

He passes me a straw and I drop it in the glass. Finally

I can hold the glass straight. It's a relief to hear that slurping sound as I drink my way down to the bottom. "That was sweet of you, Izzie," I say.

He shrugs.

I look at my little brother and now I notice the bald spot on the side of his head where they shaved his hair. I realize no one's been telling him to get well, no one's been trying to comfort him. He was in the accident too.

"I was wondering, Izzie, those stitches on your head, do they hurt?"

"Sometimes they hurt. Papi said not to complain."

"Well, you can complain to me. I promise not to tell anybody."

Izzie draws closer and whispers in my ear, "The stitches hurt a lot when I put my head down on the pillow, but then I fall asleep and I forget they hurt."

"The stitches are still fresh. But you'll be better soon."

"Roofie, it was spooky. The doctor sewed me up with a needle and thread, like I was a pair of pants."

"Wow, Izzie, you saw him?"

"Yeah, I was awake."

"Hey, Izzie . . ."

"What, Roofie?"

I remember the letter to Ramu.

"Can I ask you for a favor?"

"Yeah, sure."

"Will you give this letter to Ramu tomorrow? If you don't see him on the way to school, then give it to him in the cafeteria. Put it in his hand, okay?"

"Okay."

Izzie stuffs the letter into his pants pocket.

The next day Izzie gives Ramu my letter in the cafeteria. He comes home with something hidden inside his lunch box, a gift from Ramu.

"Quick, eat it before Mami finds out," Izzie says.

It's a samosa, with the crispy soft potato filling, and it's a bit spicy and tastes even better than the first time. As I hurry to finish the last delicious bite, I feel a sudden sadness in the pit of my stomach, knowing it will be a long time before I can give my friend Ramu a sweet guava pastry in return.

a teacher all to myself

Mrs. Sarota keeps her promise. The following week the school sends a tutor to our house who will come three times a week.

I've never had a teacher all to myself! Her name is Miss Hoffman, but she tells me to call her Joy. She's wearing bell-bottom pants and a peasant blouse with puffy sleeves, and she has shiny dangling earrings.

"You look like a hippie, not a teacher," I say.

She laughs. "You're right, I am a bit of a hippie. I believe in love, peace, and flower power. But I'm also a teacher."

"That's good," I say to Joy. "Because I don't want them to send me back to the dumb class after missing so much school!"

"That won't happen," Joy says. "Not if we keep your brain working. Being bedridden shouldn't hold you back."

"Bedridden"? The word sounds to me like a witch's curse: *And you, Ruth, will be BEDRIDDEN for the rest of your days . . .*

Mami and Joy set up a chair and table next to my bed and that becomes my classroom.

Joy arrives late in the morning, after Papi has left for work and Izzie has gone to school. Mami makes toasted Thomas' English muffins for both of us. She gives Joy a whole muffin spread with butter. I get half a muffin with a dab of butter so I don't get too fat to fit in my cast.

Joy reads out a list of words and asks me to spell each one and tell her what it means. They're easy words and I know them all.

"Far-out," Joy says after I get all the words right. "You're so smart! I'm surprised they kept you in the remedial class for so long."

I always knew I wasn't dumb!

Before she leaves, Joy gives me a book of stories by Hans Christian Andersen. She tells me to choose one story and write an explanation of what I learned from reading it. I choose "The Red Shoes."

This is what I write:

"The Red Shoes" is about a girl named Karen. Her mother dies and Karen almost starves to death. But an old woman adopts her. One day Karen gets a new pair of red shoes. Back then, good girls only wore black shoes. Red shoes were for bad girls.

The old woman gets sick, but Karen puts on the red shoes and goes to a party anyway. On the dance floor, the shoes take over. Karen can't stop dancing and she can't take off the shoes. They stick to her feet. She dances for days and days, forgetting about the old woman.

Karen learns the old woman has died. She didn't even

say good-bye to the old woman who saved her life! It was
the fault of the red shoes. An angel had put a curse on her:
"Dance in your red shoes till your skin shrivels up and you
are a skeleton!"

"Chop off my feet," she begs. And they chop them off
and the shoes keep dancing by themselves, her feet still
inside them. She cries and cries, asking for forgiveness,
until finally another angel takes pity on her. She dies and
he takes her to heaven on his wings.

I could relate to this story because having my legs in
a cast feels like they've been chopped off. I know they
haven't been. They are still there. Yes, I have legs. I just
can't see them. Or move them. Or feel them.

"Good job, Ruthie!" Joy says. "You get a gold star."

I feel happy when Joy pastes a gold star in my notebook, although I think maybe part of the reason I am getting it is because Joy feels sorry for me. She sees how hard it is for me to write lying flat on my back in bed.

I find out that it's just as hard to read lying on my back as it is to write. I have to balance my book on the edge of the cast and lift my head to see the pages.

When my neck gets tired and achy, I let my head fall on the pillow and hold the book straight above me. Then my arms get tired and achy, and I give up and stare at the ceiling.

Sometimes when my whole body aches like this, I close my eyes and pretend I am lying on my favorite beach in Cuba. It had a curious name, Playa Vaquita, which means

Little Cow Beach, and the sand was like silk. When the tide was low, long zigzagging sandbars would form. I could wade into the deep end without being afraid. The water wouldn't come any higher than my knees.

I remember laughing and running on that beach, trying to keep my kite from falling down out of the sky.

I wish I had strong legs to run on the beach with a kite. It doesn't have to be Playa Vaquita. Any beach will do.

I wish I had long arms like an octopus. I'd paste gold stars on the ceiling and imagine them twinkling day and night.

Those are my big wishes.

My small wish is to look out the window and just see the world. But the window is behind me. I can't see the sun or the clouds. I can't say "good night, moon" before going to bed. It's just the ceiling and me.

Dear God,

Thank you for sending Joy to be my teacher. She is a very nice teacher. I am learning a lot and getting smarter every day. But if I had to choose between going back to the dumb class and not being able to walk, I would ask you to send me to the dumb class.

Ruthie

if Mami stops taking care of me

Time is different when you can't leave your bed. The days go slowly because they all seem the same. Not moving, not going anywhere, always in the same place, it's hard to tell if a new day has begun or an old day has ended. So Joy gets me a calendar to keep track of the days. The months are stapled onto a piece of cardboard. I've torn off January, February, March, and April—the month the accident happened.

Four weeks in the body cast and counting. Now I know why they call sick people by the word "patient." The *patient* has to have *patience*. Wait and wait and wait and not lose hope.

It feels good to cross off the days on the calendar. When May passes, I'll tear it off and that will feel good too. And then June and July, those months will come, and they will pass, so many months. Maybe in August I will get my body cast off? I hope, I hope, I hope.

It's a Sunday morning and the sun is just coming out when I open my eyes. The light streams in from the window that's behind my bed and feels like a golden cape around my shoulders. I lie in bed, stare at the ceiling. I need to pee, but I hold it in. I don't want to bother Mami. She's sleeping and I feel bad making her get up to bring me the bedpan.

When Izzie wakes up and jumps out of bed, I close my eyes and pretend to be asleep. He rushes to the living room to wake up Mami and Papi, cuddling with them on the sofa bed until they're ready to get up. I hear them giggling and laughing. They forget all about me.

Then Mami comes rushing, like an alarm went off in her head, and she remembers she has a daughter who can't leave her bed. She brings the bedpan and a basin of water for me to wash my hands. After I'm done, she and Papi and Izzie eat breakfast in the dining room while I eat from a tray that sits on top of my cast. It's a little lonely eating by myself, but I'm getting better at balancing the tray and keeping my food from spilling all over the place.

Then Izzie comes to say good-bye. He's wearing his patched-up pants and a T-shirt, no jacket.

"Must be nice outside now."

"Yeah, it's nice," he says. "There are flowers all over the place. Too bad we can't walk on the grass or I'd bring you one."

"That's okay, Izzie. You enjoy looking at them," I say.

"I promise, Roofie, I'll look at them a lot, a lot, a lot!"

That makes me smile. I don't want him to feel sorry for me. It's not his fault I broke my leg.

"See you later, Roofie!" he says and he's out the door.

Papi comes in next. He's dressed in black slacks and a red shirt and a red cap that says "Avis Rent-a-Car."

"Where are you going, Papi?"

"I have to go to work, Ruti. Just for a couple of hours."

"Do you have a new job, Papi?"

"*Sí, mi hija,* I am starting today. I'll get to decide what cars to give people. If they don't make a face when I speak English, they'll get a nice car. If they act like they can't understand me, I'll give them the worst car they have at Avis."

Papi and I laugh.

"That's funny, Papi. But now you work every day, Monday to Sunday!"

"We need a little extra money, *mi hija*. The good thing is that in this glorious country there's plenty of work for everybody!"

He bends his head so I can give him a kiss on his cheek.

"Now give your papi a big hug."

I reach my arms up as high as I can and hug him around the neck, smelling his familiar Old Spice.

"Bye, Papi!"

Everyone is always leaving. And I am always saying goodbye since I can't go anywhere.

My bed is my island; my bed is my prison; my bed is my home.

Hands soapy from washing dishes, Mami pops her head in. "You have company! Your zeide is here."

When he appears in the doorway, I yell out, "Yay, Zeide! Come in!"

Zeide's green eyes shine when he sees me. He often brings me a gift, something unusual, like a key chain with a Gumby hanging from it, or a crinkly fan with a picture of an old-fashioned lady in an evening gown.

This time he brings me a big bottle of prune juice, pours a glass for me, and drops in a straw.

"Why are you giving me juice?" I ask.

Es muy bueno," he replies. "It will help you." He gulps down a glassful to show me how tasty it is.

"I don't want to drink that, Zeide. It doesn't look good."

"Try it, you'll like it. Just a little," he says in his whispery gentle voice.

I sip some of the prune juice just to please Zeide. But I can't get it down my throat. It's the yuckiest thing I've ever tasted.

I spit some out, and a big black blob lands on the white blouse Mami washed and ironed for me.

"Sorry, Zeide," I whimper, ready to cry. Staining my white blouse with my spit-out juice makes me feel like the grossest person in the world.

Mami comes marching in, furious. "Why didn't you drink the prune juice?" she says.

"I don't like it."

"You need to poop or you're going to explode! It's been two weeks since you've made *caca*."

"Mami, don't use that word. It's embarrassing!"

"*Caca, caca, caca.* You have to make *caca*!" she shouts.

She's gotten good at turning me on my stomach. Before I know what's happening, she's reached for the pole between my legs and flipped me over.

"Wait! Tell Zeide to leave. I don't want him to see!"

"I'm going out, Ruti, don't worry," Zeide says in his whispery gentle voice.

Mami slips something inside my butt that feels like a stick of butter.

"Stop, Mami, stop!" I scream.

"You have to poop! Everyone has to poop!"

My insides start gurgling. "Oh no, get the bedpan! Turn me around! Fast!"

Mami flips me on my back again, and I can't stop the black liquid from pouring out of my body. It's a stinky, stinky river.

"You've held it in for weeks! Why can't you wait a minute now?" Mami yells. She goes running out of the room and runs back with the bedpan.

But it's too late. The sheets will have to be changed. Mami puts the bedpan underneath me anyway.

"Change the sheets," I cry. "Mami, please!"

"I will, in a minute," Mama says and sighs as she turns to leave.

I hear Mami and Zeide talking in the living room.

"I try my best, Papá. Sometimes I just reach my limit."

"Ruti is a good girl, but she's suffering, and you're suffering too, with her."

"Papá, I know I shouldn't say this, but I feel like I'm going crazy being cooped up all day in this tiny apartment, like I am in prison."

"I know, *mi hija*, I know. But it is not Ruti's fault. She is stuck in here all day too, wishing she could walk and run like all children do."

"I don't know how we are going to survive this, Papá."

"As the saying goes, '*No hay mal que dure cien años.*'"

I translate the words I just heard: There's no pain that can last a hundred years. That better be true!

Then I hear Mami respond sadly, "I hope you're right, Papá."

I smell the sugary Cuban coffee Mami must be making, hear the china cups tinkle in their saucers. If I could, I'd run to the living room and fling the coffee cups out of their hands. But I can't do anything except lie in my poop and wait.

Finally Mami returns. She enters the room and whips the dirty sheets off the bed. She gives me a wet towel to scrub myself as she lifts me with the pole. Then she brings a basin with soap and water, and I wash my hands. Finally she puts clean sheets on the bed, stretching the cloth tightly at the four corners.

As she gathers the dirty sheets, she looks at me like I'm the most disgusting creature in the world. An animal. A pig.

"I'm sorry, Mami, I'm really sorry."

Mami doesn't answer. She walks out carrying the dirty sheets.

She doesn't come back for a long time. I am thirsty. I want water. I am lonely. But I know better than to ask Mami for anything when she's tired of me. I promise myself I won't call her even if I have to wait hours and hours.

I open up the book of Hans Christian Andersen stories and read the words I know by heart: "Far out in the ocean, where the water is as blue as the prettiest cornflower, and as clear as crystal, it is very, very deep . . ." Oh, if only I could swim in the ocean like the little mermaid, then I wouldn't mind my cast so much.

It's late in the day when Mami comes back to my room, bringing me lunch on a tray—an open-faced grilled cheese sandwich, with just one slice of bread, an apple cut in wedges, and a glass of water.

She has taken a shower and is wearing a satiny blouse the color of sea coral and a tight skirt, lipstick as red as hibiscus flowers, and high heels with open toes, as if she were going someplace fancy, not stuck at home with a daughter who can't get out of bed.

"*Gracias*, Mami," I say in my sweetest voice. "You look beautiful."

She just barely nods.

"Mami, do you still love me?"

"Of course I still love you," she snaps. She looks sadder than ever.

I know Mami has to love me. I'm her daughter. And I

wish she didn't have to be shut up in the house with me all day too.

I want her to go out. I want the world to look at her. She's too pretty to be trapped in a cage. The only problem is, if Mami leaves me, I'll die, and I don't want to die. I want to grow up. I want to travel the world and wander in sand dunes and climb to the top of snowcapped mountains. I'll visit cities that have beautiful names like Ipanema and Kyoto. I'll do so much.

Someday . . .

In the meantime, I'm just a girl going nowhere.

they come to see the little piggy in the barn

Instead of going out for a picnic in the park or a roller coaster ride in Coney Island on the weekends, the whole family comes to visit me now. So do all of Mami and Papi's old friends from Cuba. Mami leads them into the bedroom. And Izzie buzzes around, saying, "Can I show them? Let me show them!"

They come to see the little piggy in the barn. Oink, oink, I want to say as they enter. They smile for half a second. Then their faces get droopy when they have a look at me. "How are you, Ruti?" they ask, concern in their eyes.

I try to smile and act like I don't mind being stuck in bed. "I feel great," I tell them. "I'm getting to read lots of books! And I'm a whiz at crossword puzzles now!"

"Very nice, Ruti."

No one knows what else to say.

The men put their arms around the women's shoulders and edge them toward the door. They don't look back. They are relieved when they leave the icky barn where the little piggy girl lives.

I can tell Baba is the one who suffers the most when she sees me. She is still taking a pill every night to be able to sleep. If not, she has terrible nightmares and screams, "Help, help!" and wakes up Zeide.

She worries that my broken leg is all her fault because I was asleep on her lap when the accident happened. She's convinced if she'd only held on to me tighter I might not have gotten hurt.

"*Shayna maideleh, shayna maideleh,*" Baba says over and over, brushing away tears as she enters the room. I like hearing her call me "beautiful girl," but I don't like to see her cry.

I tell Baba it's not her fault. Whenever she comes, I ask her to sing to me so we can forget the bad things that have tried to rob us of our happiness.

My favorite song is a Cuban lullaby, and I love the way Baba sings it with a whisper of a Yiddish accent.

> Esta niña linda
> que nació de día
> quiere que la lleven
> a la dulcería.
> *This pretty little girl*
> *who was born by day*
> *wants to get taken*
> *to the candy store.*

"Baba, please tell me the story of how you got from Poland to Cuba."

"But you've heard that story many times," she says.

"I know, but I want to hear it again."

Baba pushes the chair closer to my bed. She takes my hand and begins telling me the story, "*Ay, ay, ay, shayna maideleh*, what a time that was. If you can imagine, I was only eighteen. It was 1925 when I said good-bye to my family and took a train from Warsaw to Rotterdam. Then I boarded a big ship."

"What was it like, Baba, to travel all by yourself? Were you very scared?"

"I was scared, of course. I had never traveled before, on either a train or a ship! The train was crowded with lots of sweaty people, but I thought for sure it would be romantic to be on a ship at sea. But no, that ship carried cows and sheep and goats and a few people. It was like Noah's ark."

"Did the trip seem very long to you?"

"Days and days at sea—I thought we'd never arrive. I missed my family and didn't know if I'd ever see them again. I was going to a strange land where I didn't know anyone. There was the ocean on all sides, endless, and the smell of salt and brine was so strong all the food tasted like a sour pickle.

"Then one day a seagull flapped its wings near us. We were close to land, and soon we reached the shores of the beautiful island of Cuba. I began a new life. I tasted fruits I never knew existed, like mango and papaya. The sweetness of pineapples seemed a gift from heaven. And the people were kind. No one said a bad word to me because I was Jewish. I met your zeide, and together we worked and brought my mamá and papá and my brothers and sisters from Poland to Cuba. We were so happy."

Baba is quiet for some time. Then she rubs her eyes, holding back the tears, not able to let go of all the sadness she carries with her.

"If we hadn't gone to Cuba, we would not be here talking today," Baba tells me. "Cuba saved us from Hitler and the war. When you were born, our first grandchild, you were a gift of hope. We thought our home would always be in Cuba . . . and then we had to leave Cuba and come here to New York. I have been a refugee not once but twice. But somehow we found the strength to start from nothing a second time."

"And now we're happy, aren't we, Baba? Like Papi says, we're in a free country."

"Oh, *shayna maideleh*, I tell you, we are—but I won't be at peace until you are out of this cast and able to walk."

I reach for the handkerchief I took away from Mami, the one from Cuba, and pass it to Baba.

"Please, Baba, don't cry. I'm going to get well. We just have to be patient like you were on that ship."

"Yes, that's right," Baba replies and gives me a smile. "Everything comes to those who wait."

Baba digs into her purse and pulls out a butterscotch candy.

"Hide it under your pillow," she whispers. She knows if Mami sees the candy, she'll take it from me.

"*Gracias*, Baba. Will you tell me the story again another day?"

"Of course, *shayna maideleh*, as many times as you want.

My life has become a story. One day your life will become a story too."

"That's going to take forever." I sigh.

"But you'll get there, *shayna maideleh*, I promise. All we can do is have faith that life leads us where it does for a reason, so we can learn things we didn't know about ourselves. One day you will look back on your suffering and you will find a meaning for it and that will be your story."

Just when I have given up wondering if Danielle will ever come to visit, I hear her at the door asking Mami, "Madame, may I say hello to Ruthie? Is she well enough to receive guests?"

"Hi, Ruthie," Danielle says as she walks into the room. "I'm sorry you can't play hopscotch."

Danielle wears a green dress with a white collar and white ankle socks and white pumps with satin bows. Her long black hair is tied into a thick braid that reaches down her back, a green bow at the end. She could not look more perfect.

"I'll be better soon," I reply, trying to sound cheerful. "Sit down, Danielle. We can play cards, if you want. Or Monopoly."

There's a chair by my bed where all the visitors sit. But Danielle doesn't sit. She stands there staring at me, shuffling her feet.

"Do you want to sign my cast?" I ask her.

I pull away the sheet from my left side, so she can have a look at how the cast stretches from my toes to my waist.

She takes a quick glance and turns pale. Then she says,

"Thank you, Ruthie. Not now. I just came to say hello. Maman said I should come and see you, that it was the polite thing to do."

I can tell she's afraid to be alone with me. Maybe she thinks I'm contagious and she'll end up in a body cast too.

She peeks at her watch. "Sorry. I have to go."

She runs out of the room like everyone else, without looking back.

After she's gone, I lie there in my plaster cast, staring at the empty spot where she had been standing.

Everyone has stopped seeing the person that I am, the girl named Ruthie. Sometimes I feel like I am little more than my plaster cast. I have to lie here and be pitied. Where do I hide? Where do I run? I feel naked to the whole world.

The only children who come over every day, without fail, are my cousins, Dennis and Lily. They skid into the bedroom with Izzie and the four of us play a round of Monopoly or Scrabble. But they're younger and babyish and quickly tire of being cooped up inside. After a few minutes, they run off and play in the street.

One afternoon after coming home from school, Dennis and Izzie toss a ball around in the room. It flies near the bed and I catch it and throw it back. I'm so happy to be a regular kid again!

"Good save, Roofie!" Izzie shouts.

He tosses the ball to Dennis, so he can then toss it over to me. We're having fun, but Lily rushes to tattle-tale on us.

Mami storms in, yelling, "*Niños*, don't play here! What if you hit Ruti's leg?"

"It's okay, Mami!" I say. "The cast is hard. The ball won't hurt me. Don't make them leave. Please!"

But Mami doesn't care what I say. She shoos the kids out of the room. "*Fuera, niños.* Go outside!"

They don't look back either. And off they go, out to where the sun is shining.

a flashlight and Nancy Drew to the rescue

What does sunshine feel like?

I can't remember.

Since the window is behind me, I see only shadows and streaks of light.

In the morning the room is pale yellow. In the evening it turns gray. And at night a black curtain falls over the world.

I ask Papi for a flashlight to make up for the sunlight I've lost. He gets me one bright enough to shine into the darkest tunnel.

I keep the flashlight next to my pillow. So I can be brave.

The scariest time is the deepest deep of night. Every lamp is turned off in the house and everyone is asleep, except me. That's when my broken leg hurts the most. I want someone to hold my hand. I want someone to say kind words to me.

But I keep quiet because I don't think I deserve any kindness. The doctor in the emergency room told me a broken leg was no big deal.

That's why I cry as quietly as I can in the deepest deep of night. There's a box of Kleenex next to my bed and I pull out tissue after tissue to mop up my tears.

Izzie sleeps and doesn't notice.

Last night when I felt scared, I came up with a great idea. I lifted the sheet over my head and turned on the flashlight and leaned it against the cast.

I felt safe, like I was camping in a tent in the woods and surrounded by whispering trees and peaceful bears, like the stories Uncle Bill tells about taking Boy Scouts to Bear Mountain.

Now I'm camping all by myself under the sheet of my bed. I hug myself and say, "You're going to be fine. You're going to be fine. You're going to be fine."

Before falling asleep I turn off the flashlight so I won't run down the battery but I keep the sheet over my head.

In the morning when Mami comes in with the bedpan she sees me all covered up.

"Ruti! Wake up!"

"I'm awake," I tell her.

I keep the sheet over my face. I'm not ready to come out of my tent.

"How can you breathe? Take that sheet off right now, or do you want me to take it off?" Mami says, already annoyed with me and the day hasn't even started.

I pull the sheet away and smile at her. "Look at me, I'm fine."

She sees the tissues scattered around. "Were you sneezing during the night?"

"Yeah, Mami."

"Must be all those flowers blooming," she says, looking out the window. "Winters are so long here in this country I thought I would never be able to wear sandals again. It is such a relief that summer is finally here." Then she looks at me sadly. "You'll wear sandals again one day too, *mi niña*. We just have to be patient."

"That's right, Mami. Everything's going to be all right."

What courage it takes for me to smile at Mami. To act as if I'm not worried at all.

On the last day of class before summer vacation, Joy brings me a pile of books. "Here you go, Ruthie," she says to me. "You can read these Nancy Drew mysteries over the summer and take a rest from math. You're all caught up, so no need to tax your brain."

I finish reading all ten Nancy Drew books by the beginning of July and then I have nothing new to read and no one to play with. Danielle hasn't come back. But who cares? She was mean. And Ramu, who's so nice, can't visit me.

One of the worst parts about being bored is that there is so much time to think about the terrible things that can happen and how you can't stop terrible things from happening if they're going to happen.

Like the night of the accident.

Those boys didn't know they were going to die when they

went to the discotheque. And I didn't know I'd wind up in a body cast.

I have so many fears. What if I don't heal? What if my leg stays broken forever? Even the ocean isn't big enough to hold all my fears.

I am scared of being scared.

Nancy Drew is never scared. That's what I like about her.

So I read the books over and over. I read them aloud like an actress onstage. No one is around to listen.

I read aloud from *The Clue of the Broken Locket*, where Nancy Drew says, "I'm all set to go! Tell me more about Henry Winch and why he's so frightened."

I change the line so Nancy Drew says, "I'm all set to go! Tell me more about Ruthie Mizrahi and why she's so frightened."

And there she comes, strawberry-haired Nancy Drew, the girl sleuth, so American and so sure of herself, wearing a round collared blouse and a pencil skirt, wielding her magnifying glass.

"Hello, Nancy Drew," I say. "I'm Ruthie Mizrahi. Won't you please solve the mystery of why the car accident happened, why I broke my leg, and why I ended up in my bed?"

Nancy Drew smiles down at me, raising an eyebrow. "It certainly sounds intriguing! And I've been longing for another case!"

And when I pretend Nancy is with me, it's not so bad. I have discovered if I only have me, myself, and I for company, I might as well be amusing.

Then, through the open windows, I hear the ice cream truck and kids squealing as they run and play in the streets.

I wish I could be out there playing hopscotch.

I wish I could blow on a dandelion puffball and see its dust scatter.

I wish I could stand in the sun and run to the ice cream truck and buy a chocolate cone and eat it really fast before it melts all over my hands.

I wish, I wish, I wish.

PART III

A Stone in My Heart

help me not to hate

Mami has convinced Papi he can watch over me before he goes to work on Saturday morning. She's going to the beauty parlor to get her hair done. She places the bedpan under me in case I have to pee or poop. My choice is either to hold it in, or sit on top of pee and poop. I decide to try to hold it in.

Papi sits on the chair next to my bed, reading a Spanish newspaper.

I'm angry having to lie there on the disgusting bedpan until Mami gets home and can't stop thinking about the car accident.

"Papi, tell me how the accident happened."

He puts down his newspaper, shakes his head. "Why don't we talk about something else, Ruti?"

"But I want to know. I was asleep."

"Look, Ruti, what happened was very simple. There were five boys who wanted to entertain themselves that night. The boy driving had never driven by himself. He snuck out of the house and took the car from the driveway without his parents realizing it. He invited his four best friends to go to a discotheque with him. They had a few drinks. On the way back, the boy was driving so fast the car went flying into the air and into our side of the highway. He killed himself and his friends, all five died. Sixteen years old, those boys. *Muchachitos*."

"Papi, aren't you furious at the boy who caused the accident? I am!"

"Your uncle Bill says he's going to get me a lawyer. He wants me to sue the boy's family. It's true we need the money to pay Dr. Friendlich, but I don't know . . ."

"Yeah, Papi. Listen to Uncle Bill. He's the *americano*—he knows."

"I'm not sure," Papi says. "We're nobody. We're refugees. We just arrived in this country. What if they send us back to Cuba?"

I feel the anger rise to my forehead, hot as a fever.

"Make them pay, Papi! Make them pay! That boy was wrong to be driving so fast. It's his own fault he died. He killed his friends too."

Papi replies, "Even good people can do bad things."

But I hate the boy who caused the accident.

I want the boy to pay for all the sadness he's caused—for killing his friends, for leaving a lady paralyzed for life, for forcing me to be stuffed into a body cast like a sausage.

I don't know what to do with my anger that burns and burns.

I am fuming inside my cast. If I could, I'd stomp my feet.

"Can you open the window, Papi?"

96

"It's open. But I'll try to open it more for you." He jiggles the window frame. "There. Is that better?"

A bit of air comes in, and I listen to the sparrows chirping.

"Are the leaves on the trees very green now?"

"Verde, verde," Papi tells me. "It seemed impossible that the leaves would come back after such a cold winter. In Cuba, we have one season all year long. But here the leaves die and they come back, *verde, verde*. It's a miracle."

I like the sound of that word, *verde*, in Spanish. It's more beautiful than the word "green" in English.

As soon as I can walk again under trees that bloom *verde, verde,* I'll try to forget I ever hated. Until then, the hate is a stone in my heart.

Mami comes home from the beauty parlor, happy and carefree, singing *"Cuando calienta el sol aquí en la playa,"* a Cuban love song about the warm sun on the beach. She looks even more beautiful than she looks every day. Papi leaves the room, and I can stop holding it all in, the pee and the poop. Finally, finally, finally, Mami takes away the bedpan.

Papi changes into his fumigator's uniform and stops to see me before he leaves.

"Ruti, be a good girl," he says, and bends down for me to hug him.

"I will, Papi."

"Don't think about the accident so much. We have to look forward, not back. You understand?"

"Okay," I say, but I know the stone is still there, inside my heart. I can feel it when I swallow.

As soon as Papi is out the door, Mami comes back lugging a bucket of water and a large basin and towels.

Mami scrubs my shoulders and the nape of my neck so hard that it hurts.

"Go easy, Mami! You're not polishing the stove," I yell.

When she is done, I wash under my arms with lots of soap.

The cast is smelly anyway. It smells worse than Izzie's dirty socks.

"Now it's time to take care of your hair," she says.

"Please, not today!"

I love my long hair that I've always worn in two ponytails. Since I can't leave my bed, Mami has been spraying my hair with dry shampoo and I've been brushing it out. But my hair isn't feeling very clean.

"Stop scratching your head! You look like a little monkey."

Mami pulls away my pillow and shoves the basin under my neck.

She wets my hair, working up a lather and then rinsing it with cups of warm water. Shampoo gets in my eyes and it stings, and my neck hurts from holding it stiffly over the basin. By the time we're done shampooing, Mami has spilled soapy water all over the floor and the bed. It's a big mess and she has to mop it all up. And I end up lying on a soggy mattress.

"This is the last time I wash that long hair of yours! Tomorrow I'm bringing my hairdresser over," she announces. "I'll ask her to cut your hair so it will be easier to wash."

"No!" I scream. "I don't want to lose my ponytails!!!"

"Do you want long dirty smelly hair or cute short clean hair like a sweet girl? Which do you want?"

"Mami, please don't take away my hair! Please! It's all that's left of my old life, when I was a normal girl who could walk and run and do what she wanted. We'll get better at washing it. Next time we won't get everything wet. I promise."

I look up with pleading eyes at Mami, but she stands over my bed shaking her head. "But, Ruti, just look at the mess we made. Look at me."

Her pretty pink dress is splotched with water stains.

The hairdresser is named Clara. She immediately cuts off my ponytails with two swipes of her scissors.

"No! Wait!" I scream.

The next thing I know she is dropping my ponytails in a plastic bag. I think she is going to sell my hair to people who make wigs and earn a lot of money.

Clara trims the hair around my head and ears until I'm practically bald. She dries it with a blow dryer. It's so short it takes no time at all.

As soon as Clara leaves, Mami brings me a hand mirror. "Don't you want to see? You look nice."

"Nice? I look like a sad orphan girl who cleans chimneys." I stare at my reflection. "Why did you do this to me, Mami? Why?"

"It's for your own good."

"I don't want to see myself like this!"

I throw the mirror across the room.

It shatters into lots of little pieces.

"You're a bad girl," Mami mutters under her breath as she goes to find a broom and dustpan.

I wish I didn't hear her say that.

She returns and bends to pick up the shards of glass. I worry she'll cut her delicate fingers and they'll bleed.

"I'm sorry, Mami."

"Seven years' bad luck," she says, shaking her head.

I watch Mami sweep and I feel sorry I'm making her work so hard.

I run my palms through what's left of my hair. I can't help it. I start crying. My ponytails are gone. My beautiful long hair is gone. The tears spill down my cheeks quietly. I have gotten good at crying without making a sound, without disturbing anyone.

But Mami notices. She comes to sit at the edge of my bed.

"Please, don't cry, *mi niña*. Your hair will grow back stronger, believe me."

"Without my ponytails, I'm the ugliest girl in the world. And I'm a bad girl too, just like you said I am."

Mami's eyes also fill with tears. "I'm sorry I said that to you, *mi niña*. Sometimes I get worn-out and I say things I shouldn't say. You are not a bad girl. You are a broken girl."

We both wipe our eyes with tissues, and Mami reaches over and hugs me. I start to feel better right away.

"You know what the doctor said, Mami? The doctor said I'm lucky because I didn't end up paralyzed for life like the lady in the car in front of us. So that makes me a lucky broken girl."

"That's right, *mi niña*. That's what you are. You're broken but you will heal. We just have to wait."

"But I won't have seven years of bad luck, will I, Mami? I'm sorry I broke the mirror."

"Don't worry, *mi niña*, that's an old wives' tale. Mirrors must have been expensive in the old days, so they made up that story to scare us."

"I really don't look ugly with short hair?"

"You look adorable. And I have an idea of how to make you look even more adorable!"

Mami rushes out of the room and comes back with a turquoise ribbon. She fashions it into a bow and pins it to the side of my hair. Then she brings me her small compact mirror.

"What do you think? Doesn't that look nice?"

"I like it, Mami, *gracias*. Do you think that by the time my hair grows back, I'll be walking again?"

"Let's pray for that, *mi niña*."

"Mami, can I tell you a secret?"

"Of course, *mi niña*."

"I hate the boy who caused the accident. He killed himself. He killed his friends. That poor lady is paralyzed for life! And look at me!"

Mami gazes at me with her sad eyes. "Try not to hate so much, *mi niña*. Maybe you'll get better faster."

Dear God,
Everyone tells me to stop hating the boy who caused the accident.

But I can't.

Do you think you can help? Maybe, while I sleep, you can come and snatch away all the hate that is like a stone in my heart? And then I'll dream I float up to the stars and hear them whispering to each other.

Ruthie

sky everywhere

Now every time Mami enters my room she sprays *agua de violetas*, violet cologne, all over me and mutters, *"¡Qué peste!"*

What a bad smell—my disgusting smell.

Not only is the cast getting moldy from my sweat, but it's beginning to cut into my flesh and leave ugly welts on my skin. Mami asks Aunt Sylvia to call Dr. Friendlich so she can speak to him in English and find out what to do.

Dr. Friendlich tells Aunt Sylvia I must be on a stricter diet. He says I'm getting welts because I've gained weight and my tummy is squished against the cast.

Tonight Mami only gives me one small bowl of spaghetti.

"Please, just a little more," I beg.

Mami shakes her head no.

After his dinner, Izzie comes running in from the dining room holding a fistful of chocolate chip cookies and making my mouth water. I think he's being as mean as Karen in the Hans Christian Andersen story. She just kept right on dancing in her red shoes while the kind old lady suffered and died.

While Izzie keeps eating before my eyes, I feel like I'm suffering and dying.

And it's all the fault of the boy who caused the car accident!

The stone grows and grows, bigger than my heart.

Finally I can tear the month of July off my calendar and it is time for the ambulance to come for me. Bobbie and Clay again!

"Hi, child," Clay says. "You're looking nice! Love that bow in your hair!"

They don't seem to notice I am smelly. Or maybe they pretend not to notice.

"You must be itching to go outside!" Bobbie says.

"Yeah, can't wait."

He and Clay strap me to the stretcher, and we go downstairs in the elevator.

Mami follows along in her high heels. *Clickety-clack, clack, clack.*

Outside, my eyes hurt from the light and the sunshine.

"I can't see!" I groan. "I'm going blind!"

Bobbie smiles. "Don't worry, kid. You haven't been outside for months. Your eyes have become sensitive."

He holds his hand in front of my face. "How many fingers?"

"Three."

He laughs in his mischievous way. "You can see fine. Squint. Now open your eyes slowly. You'll get used to it."

But the sky looks like it's everywhere, sky falling on top of me, sky surrounding me, sky resting at my feet. There's too much sky.

Clay sees I'm scared and he winks at me and says, "We'll turn on the siren, so everyone will get out of our way. That will be lots of fun, won't it, Ruthie?"

I nod. I don't want to tell him how much the sound of the siren frightens me and brings back memories of the accident.

Relief comes once Mami gets in beside me in the back of the ambulance and the doors are shut. We don't see anything then; we just feel how fast we're going, speeding down the highway from Queens to Brooklyn, the siren blaring. As the ambulance swings around a curve, Mami grabs my hand and squeezes hard.

"Don't worry, Mami," I say, feeling like I'm the grown-up.

Mami kisses my forehead. "You're a good girl. I'm sorry you have to suffer."

I wish Mami were always this nice to me.

I'm wheeled into a hospital room. Dr. Friendlich stands waiting for me. Using a big pair of scissors, he cuts the cast. I feel the cold sting of the steel blade as the pieces of plaster fall away like the husk of a coconut.

I see my legs again . . . what were once my legs . . .

They hang limp, reminding me again of my Cuban rag doll that Mami threw away. Even my left leg, which isn't broken, looks so useless I don't try to move it.

They take an X-ray and Dr. Friendlich holds it up to the light.

"Still broken," he says, shaking his head.

The nurse comes over with a needle and pokes my arm and I fall asleep.

When I wake up, I'm in a new white plaster cast. It covers my two legs and reaches to my chest, the same as before. I have a pole again, down by my ankles, so I can be turned on my stomach. The only thing that's different is the iron nail sticking out of either side of my right shin.

"It's a pin," Dr. Friendlich says. "To align the bone."

When Mami comes into the room, Dr. Friendlich announces, "Might be another four months before the bone heals."

Mami doesn't understand what the doctor said, so she asks me to translate.

"¡Ay no!" Mami exclaims after I tell her. *"Tanto tiempo, tanto tiempo."*

"My mother says that's a long time," I explain to Dr. Friendlich.

"Yes, Ruthie, it is," he says. "But you can't hurry a broken bone. If I were to let you stand up now, you'd crumple to the ground."

When we arrive at our building, Bobbie and Clay carry me out on the stretcher.

"Take a good look, kid," Bobbie says, stopping. "You're going to be indoors for another long stretch."

It is cloudy and the light no longer hurts my eyes. I turn my head this way and that, looking up and down our street.

I see cars parked bumper to bumper.

I see brick buildings, one next to the other, lined up in long sad rows.

On the pavement I see a hopscotch board drawn in red chalk.

I remember how nice my board was with the flowers I added and how fun it felt to throw a stone inside the squares and jump without losing my balance.

That was such a long time ago.

This world is a dream. This world isn't my world anymore. I shut my eyes as I get taken inside.

I am happy to return to my room, my bed, my island. And my ceiling that loves me and is always there above my head when I look up.

At least my cast is fresh and clean. Things aren't so bad, I tell myself, as I settle back into the stillness of my world.

And then there's a shy knock at the door.

"Hello, Mrs. Mizrahi, may I see Ruthie?"

It's Ramu! I hear his accent, the touch of India in his English.

"Come in, come in!" I yell from the bedroom. I am eager to see a friend.

Mami leads Ramu inside. He smiles and says, "Hello, Ruthie, how are you?"

"Not so good. I have to be in a body cast for another four months."

"I am sorry. That must be difficult to endure."

"Sit over here, Ramu. Can you stay for a little while?"

"I can only stay a few minutes. I'm not supposed to be

here, but my mother went out with Avik to the store and I was by myself and saw you being wheeled out of the ambulance and I felt bad I hadn't come to see you, so I decided to sneak over."

"So your mother still won't let you play in the neighborhood?"

"No. She's afraid we'll lose our customs and forget how to be polite and proper Bengali children. I don't know why we came here to America if we can't live like everyone else."

"Parents are funny. I can't figure mine out either. But I understand a little of how your mother feels. Wouldn't you be sad if she stopped making her delicious samosas?"

"Of course, I would be terribly sad. Just like you would be sad if your mother stopped making her delicious guava pastries."

I smile at Ramu. "But that doesn't really have anything to do with playing with the other kids. Why can't you play, then go home and be Bengali?"

"I know, Ruthie, it doesn't make any sense. Sometimes I feel I'm invisible, slipping through the streets, never getting a chance to be part of this place."

"Ramu, do you want some of Izzie's favorite chocolate chip cookies?" I ask him.

"Oh no, thank you, Ruthie. My mother would be very upset if I ate those American cookies." Ramu gets embarrassed and quickly adds, "I hope I haven't insulted you. I am sure they are excellent cookies."

"That's okay, Ramu, I can't have any right now either, or I'll get too big for my cast."

He bows his head, looks back at me bashfully. "I wish I could see you more. I just had to come and tell you I miss you and hope you get better fast. School is starting up again soon and it's no fun being in the smart class if you're not there!"

"Remember the story about the princess who couldn't cry?"

Ramu nods. "How could I forget? What a good story that was."

"I don't need an onion to cry," I tell him. "I cry all the time! And I hate crybabies!"

"Have faith, Ruthie. You'll be well soon."

Ramu removes a silver chain from his neck. The chain holds a silver pendant that's got a figure of a man with long hair who is standing on one leg and lifting the other in the air. He has many arms and they all look like they're moving.

"Take this. Maybe it will help," Ramu says. "It's our god Shiva, the dancing Shiva. He's very strong. He dances to bring goodness to the world. That's why I like him. One day you'll dance too, Ruthie. Shiva will help you."

He bends and slips it around my neck.

"Thanks, Ramu. Are you sure you don't need it?"

"No, I'm okay. You hold on to it for me."

I want Ramu to stay longer, but suddenly Mami comes rushing in.

"Ramu, I see your mother coming back with your brother. They're getting close to the building."

Ramu jumps to his feet. "Time to go. Hope I can come back another day."

"Bye, Ramu. Thanks for cheering me up."

"Bye, Ruthie. You cheered me up too!"

Dear Shiva,

I didn't know about you until today, when my friend Ramu gave me a chain with your image.

Ramu says you're a strong god, a dancing god. Please help me to get better, so I can walk again. I don't need to be able to dance, though that would be nice. Right now just walking would be enough.

Can you also help me get rid of all the hate in my heart? I am full of hate for the boy who caused the accident that has me trapped in my bed and I know that is not a good thing.

I come from a different religion. I hope you can still help me. Ramu says I should have faith and somehow I am going to try to find some.

Ruthie

a sadder story

Mami brings her ironing board into my room to keep me company while she works. She is in her flip-flops and looking comfortable in a *bata de casa*, as she calls the loose dress she wears when it is very hot and she's not expecting any guests to come and visit.

"There's no sea breeze here, like there is in Cuba," Mami complains. "Even with the windows wide-open, you can't get a breeze."

I agree a breeze would be nice. Being in the cast in summertime feels like I'm bundled in a hundred blankets.

"It isn't fair that I ended up like this," I groan.

"Nothing is fair, *mi niña*," she replies, her sad eyes filling quickly with tears. "Nothing. We all have our troubles. At least I am here to take care of you."

"*Gracias*, Mami. And you promise never to stop taking care of me?"

"I promise, *mi niña*. I know I lose my patience sometimes," she tells me. "But I'm only human, you know."

And suddenly we hear horrible screams from down the hall. A woman's screams.

"Oh no, oh no, oh no! Help! Help!"

"I better go see what's wrong. I'll just be a minute," Mami says, rushing off.

The woman is screaming, louder than before, "Help! Help! My little boy! My little boy!"

I recognize the voice: It is Mrs. Sharma's.

Sometimes you think your story is so sad that no one could have a sadder story. But now I cry, not for myself, but for Ramu and his family.

While their mother cooked dinner in the kitchen, Ramu and Avik played by an open window. A toy fell out of Avik's hand, and he reached out the window to catch it. But he leaned too far and fell.

Izzie is shaking and crying as he tells of his part in the story.

"We were playing outside, when all of a sudden we saw Avik flying in the air. Like a bird! He was holding a toy in his hand. When he landed, we saw what it was. The toy was a wind-up elephant from India. His mother came running. She was wearing one of her long gowns and she tripped and fell right next to Avik and spread her arms around him. He was all bloody. She lay there in the street holding him until the police came. Then they shooed all of us kids away."

Mami takes Izzie in her arms and hugs him, then she comes over to the bed and hugs and kisses me too. "*Ay, pobrecita*, the poor woman, how she must be suffering! Losing a child is the worst thing in the world that can happen to a mother. *Mi niña, mi niño,* I love you both so much!"

When Papi comes home, he and Mami go down the hall and knock on the door. They want to tell Mr. and Mrs. Sharma how sorry we are. They knock softly several times, but no one answers. Finally Mr. Sharma opens the door slowly. In a whisper, he says, "No visitors, please. Thank you." And he shuts the door.

Three days later, Mr. and Mrs. Sharma and Ramu pack their suitcases. They are going back to India.

Mr. and Mrs. Sharma allow Ramu to come over and say good-bye to me. He stands by my bed wearing Indian clothes, a loose tunic and wide pants. He looks even skinnier than usual, almost a scarecrow.

Ramu stretches out his hand. It feels brittle, like a dry leaf in autumn. I squeeze it lightly, out of fear that he is fragile now, that he could break from the sadness.

"My little brother is a pile of ashes. He's traveling back to India in a velvet box. We'll scatter his ashes in the Ganges River, so he will be at peace. His spirit will live on. The spirit never dies. But we are never coming back to America."

"I am sorry, Ramu. I am so, so sorry."

"I accept your sympathy, Ruthie. Please don't worry about me."

"I've been feeling sorry for myself all these months. But what you are going through is so much worse."

"Being unable to walk is terrible. And losing my brother is terrible. But we will both have to go on somehow."

"I hope things will be better for you in India."

"I hope you get back on your feet soon."

"I will never forget you, Ramu."

"And I will never forget you, Ruthie."

"Are you sure you don't want your chain back?"

"No, you hold on to god Shiva and keep asking him to help you. He is strong. I know he will listen to your prayers."

"Will you write to me from India?"

"I will try. It may be a while."

We know it is the last time we'll ever see each other. We clasp each other's hands one more time.

Ramu turns to leave and I wish I could walk him to the door.

"Bye, Ramu," I whisper.

For days and days after Ramu leaves, I think about Avik. I wonder how he felt flying in the air. Maybe he felt happy for a second before crashing to the ground—happy to be free, happy not to be locked up in the house. I hope so.

Dear Shiva,

Little Avik is on his way back to India. He was a good boy, always held his brother Ramu's hand when they crossed the street, always listened to his mother.

Please welcome him home when he arrives.

Ruthie

Chicho comes from Mexico

A new neighbor moves into the apartment down the hall where Ramu and Avik used to live. His name is Francisco, but he says to call him Chicho. He speaks a slower, more polite Spanish than our Cuban Spanish—which Papi says is always in a rush to catch a train. Chicho uses the word "*ándale*," and his voice rises and falls in a singsong way that cheers you up.

Mami and Papi make friends right away. They are glad to have a neighbor they can talk to in Spanish and they tell him he's always welcome to come over for a Cuban coffee. The last two evenings, after dinner, he has stopped by. He is so boisterous I can hear everything he says from the bedroom.

"All my family is in Mexico. I'll never go back there to live, only to visit. I think New York is the best city in the world! Don't you? Here you can be what you want and no one bothers you. I can step out into the street wearing a pineapple on my head and no one will bat an eye! Isn't that wonderful?"

He makes Mami and Papi laugh out loud with all his

stories. I'm jealous I can't be in the living room, so I call out to Mami to bring me the bedpan.

"Mami, can you bring it now?"

I hear Mami explain to Chicho, "It's our daughter. She's in bed with a broken leg."

"Oh no, *pobrecita*, why didn't you tell me?" he says. "Can I meet her?"

"Let me bring her the bedpan first. Then you can meet her," Mami says.

When Mami comes in with the bedpan, I tell her I changed my mind.

"Ruti, don't do that again," she snaps at me. "Call me when you really need the bedpan or I won't bring it to you anymore."

She leaves the room and I'm afraid she won't bring Chicho in after that, but a minute later she leads him in.

"She's been in bed for over four months," Mami says to him, as if I can't talk for myself. "The doctor says she'll have to be in bed another four." Then she lifts the covers in one swoop. She lets him gaze at the cast on my legs and at the pole between my ankles. I feel like I'm her freak-show daughter.

But Chicho looks me straight in the eyes and I can tell that he commiserates with me. He rubs the corners of his dark eyes and pushes back his thick black hair that stands on end.

"You want to sign my cast?" I ask him.

"*Mi amor*, could I make a picture for you instead?"

"Please, yes, a picture!" I say eagerly.

"Okay, just a minute, and I'll get started."

He runs to his apartment and brings a wooden box filled with paints in many different colors and a few small jars of water.

"This might take a little while," he says. He smiles and starts arranging the paints and brushes along the edge of my bed.

"No rush, I'm not going anywhere," I reply.

He glances at me. "*Ay corazón*, that's so sad, it's funny."

Chicho sits by the edge of my bed. He starts by painting long green vines that sprout pink and purple flowers. They crawl up my left leg and up my right leg.

Izzie comes back up from playing outside and watches as Chicho paints my cast.

"Wow, you're good!" Izzie says to Chicho.

"*Gracias, niño, gracias,*" Chicho replies and continues painting.

And then Izzie gets bored standing around and goes outside again.

I don't get bored. I love watching Chicho paint. He mixes colors and applies them to my cast as if I were a canvas.

"Are you getting tired yet?" I ask Chicho.

"No, *mi amor*. But I could use another cup of your mother's delicious Cuban coffee."

"Okay, I'll get it for you." I yell out, "Mami! Chicho wants more coffee!"

"Coming, coming!" Mami responds and brings the coffee to Chicho in one of her tiny porcelain cups.

He enjoys every sip. "*Gracias*, Señora Rebeca. *¡Qué rico!*"

Then Chicho paints delicate butterflies fluttering with lacy wings and tiny birds with long beaks that he says are hummingbirds. After a long while, he puts down his brushes and smiles.

"Now we have to wait for the paint to dry."

I look down my cast, trying to see everything that Chicho has painted, but since I can't sit up, it's hard for me to take it all in.

"Let me bring you a big mirror," Chicho says. "So you can see better."

Again he runs back to his apartment and comes back with a full-length mirror that he holds at my feet. In the mirror I see all the details: the vines, the flowers, the butterflies, and the hummingbirds in lots of colors.

"Thank you, Chicho! It's so beautiful!"

"I'm glad you like it."

"You paint in a psychedelic way. My teacher is going to love it," I tell him, and I'm proud of myself for using that grown-up word.

Chicho laughs and his dark eyes twinkle. "It's the effect of your mother's Cuban coffee!"

By the time he's done painting, it's nighttime. Mami sets the table for dinner, and Papi invites Chicho to stay and eat with them and Izzie. But Chicho says, "Can I eat in the bedroom with Ruti? That will be fun. An indoor picnic!"

Mami brings him dinner on a tray, just like she brings for me. She gives Chicho a huge helping of black beans and a huge mound of white rice and fried steak smothered with fried onions, and an entire plate of sweet fried plantains.

I have to stay on my diet so I won't burst out of my cast. I only get a little bit of each thing and not even one fried plantain. But as soon as Mami leaves the room, Chicho gives me one of his. "Eat quickly, *ándale, niña,*" he says.

"Are you an artist, Chicho?" I ask.

"I wanted to be an artist, but my papá wouldn't let me. He said it wasn't a good career for a young man. So I became an engineer. I specialize in bridges. But at night, I take out my paints and make pictures. Just for myself."

"I'd like to make pictures too," I tell Chicho. "I used to make pictures with chalk on the sidewalk, to decorate my hopscotch. And I was always drawing and painting when we lived in Cuba. But here I don't have any supplies. They cost too much."

He squeezes my hand. "Really? Would you like some paints and paper?"

"Yes, yes!"

"I'll come tomorrow and bring you all the art supplies you need to get started. *¿Está bien, mi amor?*"

"*Sí, sí!*"

"*Ándale, pues. Hasta mañana.*"

The next day, Chicho returns with paper, paints, and brushes. He also brings along a special easel he made himself, with wood and hinges. Under his arm he carries two very thick pillows.

"Rest your easel on your belly. That's it, *amorcito.* Now get close to the paper. With your head supported by these pillows, you won't strain your neck."

"This is perfect, Chicho! *Gracias, gracias.*"

"*Ándale*, you don't have to thank me. We're neighbors and that's what neighbors are for, to help each other."

"Can you show me how to paint, Chicho?"

"I can't show you how to paint, but I can show you how to use the art supplies. This is how you hold the brush, lightly, between your fingers. Then you dip it in the paint. Don't feel limited by the primary colors. Make up your own colors. Here are a few plastic cups on this tray, so you can mix up the colors. Experiment! See what happens when you mix blue and yellow, red and white."

I am happy to have the paints and brushes, but I know Mami isn't going to want to clean up after me. She already has enough to do taking care of the bedpan routine and having to look after me day after day.

Chicho notices the change in my mood. "Why do you look so sad, *amorcito*? Are you not excited about being an artist anymore?"

"It's going to be too messy. You know, I won't be able to clean the brushes."

"Don't worry, *niñita*, I'll clean the brushes for you. I'll make sure everything stays neat and tidy. When you're done, just leave the brushes in this jar. It has a little water in it, so the brushes won't dry up. I'll gather them each day and bring them back, ready for you to paint again."

"Chicho, this is so nice of you."

"To tell you the truth, I am being a little selfish, *mi cielo*. I want you to become the artist I couldn't be."

"But you still are an artist, Chicho!"

"Only for myself, and maybe that is enough . . ." He smiles and pushes back his hair, standing on end as usual. "Well, *mi niña*, shall I leave you alone now, so you can paint? Artists need to be quiet so they can hear the stories inside their hearts."

"Okay, but before you go, can I tell you something, Chicho? It's important."

"Tell me. Do you want to whisper it in my ear?"

"Yes."

Chicho comes closer and brings his face next to mine.

"Tell me. I am ready."

"The apartment where you live, a family from India used to live there. The mother liked sandalwood incense and the father was always working. And there were two boys. One is named Ramu and he was my friend in school. The other boy, his younger brother, was named Avik. Poor little Avik."

I start to cry, but quietly, in the way I've learned to cry since the accident.

"*Ay no. ¿Qué pasó, mi niña?*"

"Little Avik . . . He was playing by the window. He fell and he died."

"How terrible, terrible."

"And Ramu went back to India with his mother and father. He says they'll never come back to America . . ."

"*Ay no*, and he was your friend?"

"He was a friend from when we were both in the dumb class. We were in the dumb class just because we didn't know English."

"How unfair."

121

"And Ramu gave me this necklace before he left. See? It's the god Shiva, the dancing god. Ramu told me he's very powerful."

"How beautiful of Ramu to give it to you as a souvenir."

"Chicho!! How did you know to say that word 'souvenir'? That's the word Ramu had to be able to spell to get out of the dumb class! And I had to spell the word 'commiserate.'"

"What wonderful words! Life is full of surprises. Our paths cross in the most unexpected ways. It's all very mysterious."

"But, Chicho, why did Avik have to die? He was a good boy."

"No one can answer that question, *mi niña*. Some of us come here as shooting stars, to shine brightly for only the briefest moment, and others of us come and overstay our welcome, living to a ripe old age and forgetting our own names."

I don't want to be sad any longer. I reach for the brush and the paints.

"Okay, what should I paint, Chicho?"

"I have an idea, *mi niña*. Will you make a picture of Avik for me? You see, I have an altar in my apartment. It's a Mexican tradition to have an altar with flowers and candles and pictures of your ancestors and of people who have died whose souls need to find peace and tranquility. Make me a picture of Avik and I will add it to my altar. I will dedicate a special candle to him, to Avik, the little boy who lived in my house before I arrived, and I will burn sandalwood incense for him too. That way we'll never forget him."

"Chicho, I will make a picture of Avik for you right now."

I set the paper on the easel and get to work. It doesn't take too long before Avik appears, with his wide brown eyes, holding the wind-up elephant in both hands, so it won't get lost. I look at the picture for a moment before I pass it to Chicho and realize one thing is missing. He needs wings. So I give Avik some wings. That way he can fly as much as he wants in heaven.

Frida, the guardian angel of wounded artists

Now I paint every day.

I make pictures of myself in bed in the cast. I make the cast look different in each picture. I am an Egyptian mummy in one picture. In another picture, I give myself a fish tail like a mermaid. I make a picture where Mami stands next to me with the bedpan. I make a picture of Izzie eating chocolate chip cookies as the tears pour down my face. I make a picture of Papi gathering me in his arms after the accident, my broken leg dangling, and the Oldsmobile bursting into flames behind us. There's a picture of Baba sitting next to my bed and singing to me and I am smiling. I even make a picture of Zeide holding up a bottle of prune juice as if it were a trophy (ever since that day, I drink a little prune juice every morning, and Zeide was right, it tastes pretty good once you get used to it).

I make a picture of Joy to welcome her back when summer vacation is over. I paint her in her bell-bottom pants and puffy-sleeved blouse with a halo of flowers and a pink peace sign in her hands.

"Thank you, thank you, Ruthie!" she exclaims. "That is the most beautiful portrait anyone has ever made of me."

"I'm glad you like it, Joy. It's yours to keep."

"I will treasure it, Ruthie."

Again I feel so thankful to have Joy as my teacher. But then I can't help it, I suddenly feel like I want to cry.

"You are the best teacher in the world. But, Joy, I don't know—"

"What's the matter, Ruthie?"

"It's a whole new school year and I miss going to school. I miss not being with other kids. How will I ever catch up with everyone?"

"Oh, sweetheart, I know it's difficult being out of school, but believe me, you will be fine one day, and then you will go back to being a regular kid."

"But I've forgotten how to be a regular kid. I don't know what it's like to be free to be able to walk to school and play outside. I'm like a turtle now, stuck in its shell."

"Don't you worry," Joy says. "A leg doesn't stay broken forever. Everything will come naturally as soon as you are healed."

"I hope that is true," I tell Joy. "I wish I were as brave as my grandmother, my baba. She had to leave everything behind and took a ship and crossed the ocean all by herself. Baba landed in Cuba and met my grandfather, my zeide, and worked to bring the whole family to Cuba before Hitler could hurt them. Isn't that amazing?"

"Yes, Ruthie. Very amazing! Your grandmother would have gotten along well with Emma Lazarus. She was also a brave woman."

"Who's she?"

"She was a writer and a poet. She wrote a poem that is engraved on the Statue of Liberty that says, 'Give me your tired, your poor, your huddled masses yearning to breathe free.'"

Joy tells me that Emma Lazarus came from a Jewish family, and that her ancestors were immigrants from many places, and they too lost countries more than once, like in my family.

"Maybe because her family moved around so much, Emma Lazarus fought for the rights of immigrants. She also fought for religious freedom. Even though she herself wasn't religious. She felt God was in the earth we stand upon, in the trees that give us shade, in the goodness in our hearts."

"So, Joy, it's okay that even though I'm Jewish, I sometimes pray to other gods?" I ask her.

"That's all right, Ruthie. We have freedom of belief here in America. And freedom of expression too."

"I know. My father is always saying this is a glorious country because it's a free country."

"And we have to keep working to make sure it's free for everyone. But freedom can mean many different things. That's your homework—I want you to think about what freedom means to you, Ruthie, and then in our next class we'll have a debate so you can consider all the arguments and why they are significant."

I love how Joy talks to me like I'm a grown-up. It's overwhelming sometimes, but she makes me think about important things I would never think about, and then I don't feel so bad that I'm stuck in bed and can't go to school like all the regular kids.

Chicho makes me think big, interesting thoughts too. Every night after work he visits me and looks at the pictures I've painted.

"This is good. And this is good too. And this one, how beautiful!"

"Chicho, aren't there any pictures you don't like?"

"What can I do? I adore them all!" he says. "You remind me of a great Mexican artist. Like you, she was in bed a long time and couldn't walk. She was in pain always, but she didn't become her pain. She still made pictures. Her name was Frida Kahlo."

He shows me some pictures in a Mexican magazine. Frida Kahlo has thick black eyebrows and eyes that can see into your heart.

"Frida turned herself into the subject of her paintings. She made self-portraits."

One picture shows a column running from Frida's chin down to her waist. The column is broken and sits in a river of blood. She has white straps encircling her belly and binding her above and below her chest. That's the tape that holds her together and keeps her from falling to pieces.

"Frida broke her back in a bus accident," Chicho explains. "Before that, she had polio. Her right leg was shorter than her left. She wore long skirts to cover her legs. Eventually they had to amputate her right leg."

"Amputate? What does that mean, Chicho?"

"The leg became infected. The doctors had to cut it off to save her life."

I can't help gasping when he says that. I tell Chicho, "I hope the doctor won't have to cut off my leg."

Chicho reassures me, "Don't worry, *mi cielo*, you'll be fine. Frida lived in Mexico a long time ago. We are in America. Medicine is very advanced here."

I know he says that to make me feel better. But I might grow up to be like Frida, one leg shorter than the other. Maybe I'll lose my leg too and I'll wear long skirts. But I'll keep making pictures . . .

Will that make me happy?

Suddenly I change my mind about wanting to be like Frida. I push away the pile of paintings I've just shown to Chicho.

"What's wrong?" Chicho asks.

"Chicho, I want to be an artist, but I also want to be a normal girl. I want to run around and play and go to the bathroom by myself."

"I know, *mi cielo*. Don't despair. *Hay más tiempo que vida.*"

"What does that mean—'there's more time than life'? I don't get it."

"You have to be patient. Your time will come. Meanwhile, keep making pictures. Frida is gazing at you from the sky and she's happy you're drawing in bed, just like she used to do. She wants you to get well. She knows you are resilient too. Whenever you feel sad, remember you're not alone. Frida is there to help you. Frida is the guardian angel of all wounded artists and she'll always be with you."

Dear Frida,

You are a very special guardian angel to me. I am grateful to you for showing the world you can be a great artist even when you can't get out of bed.

Please make me well. Heal my legs. And I promise I'll keep painting forever.

And if you can't heal me, I'll still keep painting forever. I really love painting!

But try to heal me. Okay, Frida? Not just for my sake, but so my pretty mami can go out and stroll around in her high heels and be admired by everybody.

Thank you,

Ruthie

applause, applause

Izzie is a pirate with a black patch over one eye for Halloween. Dennis has on a sailor suit. Lily is a gypsy, with big hoop earrings she's borrowed from Aunt Sylvia and a wide multicolored skirt.

I am so jealous! If only I could go. I don't even have to dress up. I'm already in costume. I'm a mummy with a painted plaster cast!

Just before they all leave, Izzie announces, "We're going to trick-or-treat in all the buildings on our street. We'll get so much candy it will last months! Maybe years!"

"Yeah, that's great, Izzie," I say, trying not to sound too bitter.

He looks at me guiltily. "Sorry, Roofie." Then he brightens, the way he does when he gets an idea. "Wait, I know what I can do! I'll trick-or-treat for you!"

"How will you do that?" I ask.

He dashes out of the room and bounces back with another brown bag.

"Here, Ruthie, write your name on it and that will be for your candy."

I do as Izzie asks, but it makes me even sadder to think I am now a ghost, an absent girl, nothing but a brown bag with a name on it.

Two hours later, Izzie comes back with his bag brimming with candy. But my bag is only half full.

Izzie stomps his feet in fury. "People thought I was telling a lie to get more candy for myself! I told them, 'You want to see my sister? She's in a body cast in bed.' But they just laughed and said, 'Yeah, sure, take me over to see her.'"

Poor Izzie. He's trying to be good.

I take one piece and tell him he can keep the rest of my candy since I know Mami won't allow me to eat it anyway.

"Really?" he asks. His eyes light up.

I say, "Sure. It's all yours."

He comes to the side of my bed and kisses my cheek. "Thanks, Roofie. You're the best sister!" He rummages through the candy, enjoying being in charge of the extra bounty, but then he becomes downcast and says, "Roofie, if I take your candy, all those people who thought I was a liar, just pretending to be trick-or-treating for you, will be right. I don't want to be a crook."

"But you were trick-or-treating for me, that's no lie!" I tell him. "And now I'm giving the candy to you."

"Nah, Roofie. If I keep your candy, I'll be the wicked boy they think I am."

"Why not give the candy away if you don't want it?"

"Okay! But who do I give it to?"

"I know. Tomorrow, when you go to school, give the candy to the kids in the dumb class. And tell them I say hello."

"I will, Roofie. That's a great idea. I bet they'll be so happy."

I smile at him proudly. "Izzie, you really are a good boy."

"Sort of," he mutters, looking unsure of himself. "I don't know. Mami is always scolding me."

"Come on, you are." I clap my hands for him. "Bravo, Izzie! Yay!"

"Ssshhh, Roofie. I don't deserve that."

His bangs are still crooked, but my little brother is growing up.

I ate only one candy from the Halloween bag, but I can't stop worrying about outgrowing my body cast. I try to figure out some exercises to do even though I'm squished into this silly thing.

I can move my head left and right against my pillow.

I can lift my shoulders up and down.

I can punch the air with my fists.

I can clap my hands.

Mami hears me clapping my hands and comes running, thinking I want something.

"Sorry, Mami, I wasn't calling you. Just doing some exercise."

"Would you mind not clapping unless you need me?"

"Sure, Mami, sure."

At night, when Papi is back and he and Mami and Izzie have finished eating dinner, I forget and start clapping my hands again.

Papi comes in and says, "So I hear this is your new exercise routine! How about if I teach you how to clap out the beat to the cha-cha-cha?"

"I sort of remember it. How does it go again?"

"It's a nice beat—one, two . . . s-l-o-w-l-y . . . and then cha-cha-cha real quick. Your mother and I used to dance the cha-cha-cha all the time in Cuba."

"Can you show me how you danced?" I ask.

He looks at me with pity. "Let's wait until you're better."

"But I want to see you dance," I say. "Please."

"*Ven*, Rebeca," he calls to my mother. "Let's show Ruti the cha-cha-cha."

She and Papi look so happy as they sing together, *"Cha-cha-cha, qué rico cha-cha-cha,"* and dance around. I like how they shuffle their feet.

Finally they stop. They're sweating and laughing.

"That was so much fun," Mami says to Papi.

Papi takes Mami in his arms and lifts her into the air. Her wide skirt opens like a beach umbrella. *"Mi cielo,* you're as good a dancer as you were in Cuba."

I clap for them. They're so beautiful when Papi is not upset and Mami is not sad or bored.

Applause, applause!

birthday wish

I keep willing myself to be happy, but there are days when the sadness arrives and sits on my head. It gets comfortable and stays there. Like a dark cloud that won't go away,

That's what's going on this cold November day that's so rainy it feels like nighttime in the middle of the afternoon. And today isn't just an ordinary day. Today is my birthday! That should make me happy. Lots of people are coming over and we're going to have a big party. For me! For my birthday! I'm going to be eleven years old! A whole decade plus a year of being alive on Planet Earth!

But that dark cloud is sitting on my head. Go away! Go away! Go away!

Mami comes in and takes away the bedpan and then she comes back with clean water and soap and a basin. I wash my hands and say to her, "Why did you give birth to me in November? It's such a gloomy time of year."

"In Cuba it's good to be born in November," Mami replies. "By that time of year, there are no hurricanes. The breezes are soft by then, like a gentle caress."

"Do you miss Cuba all the time, Mami?"

"Not all the time," she says. "And you, Ruti, do you miss it, or have you forgotten about our island?"

"I miss Cuba, Mami. I think about Caro too. She was such a good nanny. I remember when she took me to her hometown in the countryside and I got to help gather the eggs the hens had just laid. And I remember she came to the airport to say good-bye to us when we left Cuba. Do you think she still remembers us?"

"Don't worry, *mi niña*, she remembers all of us very well. I've been writing to Caro ever since we got here."

"You have?"

"Of course, *mi niña*. The letters take a long time going back and forth, but Caro knows all about your broken leg. She has gone to the shrine of San Lázaro to pray for you, so you'll be able to walk again. He is a powerful saint. In Cuba, we also call him by the African name of Babalu-Ayé. He helps people who are suffering from illnesses and ailments of the legs."

"But, Mami, will that help me since we are Jewish?"

"*Mi niña*, yes. I believe we should accept all actions that are carried out in good faith and with a loving heart."

"Yes, Mami, I do too," I tell her. I touch my dancing Shiva necklace and remember Ramu's kindness.

I choose one of my favorite pictures to send to Caro—a picture of Mami and Papi dancing the cha-cha-cha. On the back I write to her in Spanish: *"Te quiero, Caro."*

Then Mami addresses the envelope, and I see her write the words "Havana, Cuba" in big letters.

As she puts down her pen, Mami looks sad again. Luckily, just then, there's a knock on the door and it's Chicho.

"You're early," I hear her tell Chicho. "The party for Ruti isn't until tonight."

"I came early to decorate Ruti's room. This is Mark. He came to give me a hand."

"Come in, come in! Ruti will be so happy!" Mami says, cheering up. She loves a party and it's been a long time since we've had one.

Mark has a twinkle in his eye like Chicho, but he is twice as tall and used to be a football player when he was in college. Now he's a nurse at a hospital.

"I didn't know men could be nurses," I say.

"There's not too many of us," Mark replies. "But here I am."

"Would you like pink and red balloons?" Chicho asks.

"Yes, yes!"

Chicho and Mark string the balloons together and Mark hangs them from the ceiling.

"How about pink and red carnations?"

"Yes, yes!"

Around my bed, they tuck the pink and red carnations. Then Chicho places a tiara on my head, my first ever, with sparkly crystals.

"We officially proclaim you the birthday queen!" Chicho says.

"The queen of Queens!" Mark says.

I'm happy again. The tiara has sent the dark cloud away.

⁂

By the time all the guests arrive, Mami has prepared a feast. She makes Cuban *croquetas* out of chicken rather than pork since we don't eat pork. She also prepares her famous *enrolladitos*, swirls of bread filled with a blend of tuna fish, ketchup, and cream cheese, with an olive in the center. She bakes her *pastelitos de guayaba*, the guava filling so gooey and sticky and sweet. And last but not least, she makes my favorite chocolate cake, decorated with M&M's.

The bedroom fills with people eating, talking, and laughing. What a crowd!

Baba and Zeide, Uncle Bill and Aunt Sylvia, and Dennis and Lily all come, of course.

Abuelo and Abuela, my other grandparents, who are Papi's parents, make the long trip from Canarsie in a taxi. They live close to old friends from Cuba, and don't speak English and don't speak Yiddish like Baba and Zeide. They are Turkish and speak an old beautiful Spanish from Spain, because that's where Papi's family came from long ago. We don't see Abuelo and Abuela very much because they haven't found their way in America and are afraid to get lost if they wander too far from Canarsie. But today they came for my birthday—and to cheer me up, they bring along their two yellow songbirds in their cage, Coqueta and El Flaquito, so they'll sing for everyone at the party.

"*Para alegrar la caza,*" Abuela says in her merry voice, pronouncing *casa* with a *z* instead of an *s*.

"*Gracias,* Abuela!" I say.

And she replies, "Rutica, Rutica, Rutica," which is how she calls me in that Spanish that is so old and so beautiful.

Gladys and Oscar and baby Rosa, who's now walking, have come from Staten Island. I wish Gladys wouldn't look at me so pityingly. She feels guilty the accident happened after we went to visit them.

Mami and Papi's closest friends from El Grupo also come, arriving all at once and shouting *"Hola"* to each other and smacking kisses on each other's cheeks so loudly I can hear them from my room. Like us, they are Cuban and Jewish—they dance the cha-cha-cha, and eat matzo on Passover. There's pretty, petite Mimi and her much older husband, Bernardo, and their children, Amaryllis and Abie, who go to yeshiva and know all the Hebrew prayers. Dorita, in an elegant white pantsuit, and Natan, who's very smart and an architect, are with their children, Beby and Freddy, the four of them suntanned from a weekend in Miami Beach. And there's Hilda, who is always worried Imre will be robbed because he sells diamond rings on Forty-Seventh Street, and their children, Eva and Ezra, who are too shy to talk.

The kids play card games on the floor and eat potato chips until they get bored. Then they start running around the apartment, pulling down the balloons and competing to see who can pop more of them. In five minutes, they've burst every single balloon.

Then it's time for me to blow out the candles on my birthday cake. Everyone sings "Happy Birthday," in Spanish and English. Abuelo and Abuela's songbirds, Coqueta and El Flaquito, sing too, happy to be together in their cage.

Finally they all yell, "Make a wish!"

But what should I wish for? I wish, I wish, I wish . . . I could stand on my own two feet and walk again?

Izzie screams, "Hurry, Roofie! Blow out the candles before the cake melts!"

I take a deep breath, and an image flashes before my eyes of the five young men who died in the accident. The *muchachitos*, as Papi called them. They'll never celebrate another birthday. They're dead.

I am filled with sadness for them.

At the last minute I change my wish: All I want is to be alive next year.

Being alive is the best gift of all.

Thank you, life.

please take care of these *muchachitos* in the next world

Every night I lie in bed and think about the dead *muchachitos*. The days pass, the weeks pass, and it is December. I imagine them in their cold graves, calling out to their mothers and fathers, "Don't forget our birthdays! Celebrate for us. Eat cake for us." The boy who caused the accident doesn't ask to be remembered. He bows his head and says, "Forget me, forget me."

I make lots of pictures of the five boys. I use brown and gray paint. They are the gloomiest pictures I've ever made, the faces of the boys all blurry and ghostly.

Chicho looks worried when he sees my pictures.

"Are you feeling okay, Ruti?" he asks, looking straight into my eyes.

"I'm fine," I whisper.

But he doesn't believe me.

"I know what you need—a new perspective. Let's turn your bed around, so you can see what's on the other side."

When he tells Mami what he's going to do, she gets upset

and tells him that the doctor told her and Papi not to move me. Chicho says he isn't going to move me, just the bed. "But the bed is heavy," Mami says, looking worried. Chicho tells her Mark is strong and between the two of them they can move the bed.

Mark comes over, and he and Chicho pick up the bed and turn it around.

Suddenly I can look out the window! See the snow falling! See the sun shining! See the night coming!

My spirit rises, light as a feather, to the wide sky.

Chicho checks in on me the next day. My bed is a huge mess of paints, sheets of paper, and brushes.

I show Chicho my new paintings, ablaze with bright colors. A field of green grass dotted with yellow dandelions. A sailboat floating on the bright blue sea. A huge butterfly flapping its pink and purple wings.

His eyes twinkle. "Do you feel better?" he asks.

"Much better."

"You see, life is about putting things in perspective," he tells me.

Before, I didn't know about perspective. Now I know it can change how you see the whole world.

I am also learning that I can feel two very different feelings at the same time. I am still sad about the dead *muchachitos*, very sad. But I am happy, very happy, that I can look out my window and see all the beauty that's still there, waiting for me.

❋❋❋

The next morning, when Mami brings me the bedpan, I tell her, "I want to see the newspaper that Uncle Bill kept, where they wrote about the accident."

"But why, *mi niña*? Let's put that in the past."

"I need it, Mami. I need to learn the names of the boys who died."

"All right, I will show it to you. But I don't want you to be sad again."

"It won't make me sad, Mami. I think the stone in my heart is dissolving."

In the newspaper, the boys' names are listed: Jack, Johnny, Andy, Stuart, and the boy who was driving and caused the accident, his name was Eddy.

"Mami, tell me, did Uncle Bill end up getting us a lawyer so we could sue the families of the boys who caused the accident?"

"How do you know about that, *mi niña*?"

"Papi told me."

"Well, if Papi told you, then I can tell you the rest of the story. Yes, your uncle Bill called a lawyer for us and the lawyer said we had a very strong case. But Papi decided not to do anything. We feel bad because all those boys are dead. Their families are suffering. Why punish them even more? Papi said he preferred to just work hard and pay the bills."

"Oh, Mami, I'm so glad! That's how I feel too."

"That's good, *mi niña*, that's good."

Dear God, Dear Shiva, and Dear Frida,

As you can tell, I'm not very good at praying. I haven't prayed in a long time. But today I want to pray to all three of you.

I want to say I am sorry for hating the boys who caused the accident. Their names are Jack, Johnny, Andy, Stuart, and Eddy. I hated them for too long. They were boys who made a mistake that cost them their lives and that is so sad.

Please take care of these muchachitos *in the next world. Especially Eddy needs to feel some love. He's the one who was driving the car when he wasn't supposed to. He's the one who caused the accident. He thinks he doesn't deserve any kindness. He wants to be lost and never found again. But I forgive him. So please, if you can, help him.*

Help Eddy to rest in peace.

> *Thank you,*
> *Ruthie*

a white rose in July or January

Well, Ruthie, you probably know every Nancy Drew book by heart," Joy says to me, laughing. When she laughs, it makes her dangling earrings jingle and she looks so beautiful it makes me happy.

It is our last day of classes before the holiday break and we linger over our English muffins.

"I've brought some new books for you," Joy says. "Here's a book of poems by a woman who never left her house. Her name was Emily Dickinson. She kept her poems hidden under her bed, afraid they weren't good enough. Don't worry if you can't understand all of them. Enjoy the music of her words."

"Okay, I'll try."

Joy goes on excitedly, "And since you know Spanish, I'd like you to read these poems by José Martí. He was the great independence leader of Cuba."

"Joy, I know about José Martí. In school in Cuba, we had to memorize his poem about the white rose. I still remember how it starts—*Cultivo una rosa blanca 'en julio como en enero' para el amigo sincero . . .*"

"Very good, Ruthie," Joy says. "How would you say that in English?"

"I have a white rose to tend . . . in July or January . . . I give it to my true friend," I tell Joy. "I forgot the rest of the words in Spanish, but I remember he talks about a cruel friend who breaks his heart and how he will give that friend a white rose too."

"Wow, that is just so, so, so, so amazing!" Joy replies. And her earrings jingle again.

"I wish I could be as good and forgiving as José Martí wants us to be."

"We just need to keep trying, Ruthie. That's all we can do. And you know something? You are an amazing translator!"

"I used to translate for my mother when we did the grocery shopping. Now I can't anymore."

"How about if you read the English translations of these poems by José Martí and then you can tell me if you think they capture the spirit of the original Spanish? It's a bilingual edition, Spanish on one side and English on the other. Isn't that nice? And here's a Spanish-English dictionary, in case you need it."

"Thanks, Joy. That will be fun homework. They put me in the dumb class because I couldn't speak English. But now I can speak both English and Spanish!"

"You are very fortunate to know two languages. Not everybody has that gift." She smiles and enthusiastically pulls out another book from her bag. "And I think you will love *Alice's Adventures in Wonderland* and see a lot of yourself in Alice and a lot of Alice in you. In a way, you too are on a journey into a mysterious wonderland, even though you haven't left your bed."

"I'll read them all! Thank you so much, Joy!"

"It's my pleasure," Joy says. "You're doing so well with all your reading! I bet you're at least at a tenth-grade level. I'm impressed by all the progress you've made. You haven't wasted any time while you've been bedridden."

Then she places all the books next to me, very carefully, like they are precious rubies she is entrusting to me. Now books keep me company the way my Cuban rag doll once did.

I love that Joy is helping me to become so smart!

"Joy, I'm going to miss you during the break."

"And I'll miss you too, Ruthie. Before we end class today, what do you say we see what news there is in the *New York Times*?"

"Okay, but isn't that newspaper too hard for kids to understand?"

"I think you can handle it. I've brought today's paper and one I saved for us to look at. But first let me show you how to hold the newspaper. It can be a little hard to manage."

"It's hard to manage when you're sitting, I'm sure it will be a breeze if you're flat on your back," I say.

"Oh, Ruthie, you have such a wry sense of humor." She stretches out the newspaper lengthwise and folds it in thirds. "See what I did? If you fold it like this you can follow a story that starts on the front page and finishes on an inside page. Would you like to try?"

"Sure."

I'm a little clumsy at first, but after a while I get the swing of it, though I end up with newsprint all over my fingers as we read some stories.

Then she passes me the saved newspaper from August 6, 1966, and tells me, "There's an article about Dr. Martin Luther King I think you should read. Do you know what he's fighting for?"

"Yes I do. He thinks white people and black people should be equal and able to live in the same neighborhoods and go to the same schools."

"And I agree with him, Ruthie."

Joy lowers her voice, as if she's scared to talk out loud, even though the only people in the house besides her are Mami and me.

"Why are you whispering, Joy?"

"Because a lot of white people don't feel the way I do. And I'm not supposed to share my personal opinions with my students. I could get into trouble."

I read about Dr. King going to Chicago to protest segregated neighborhoods and being attacked by a mob of angry white people who threw rocks at him. Some of the people were wearing Nazi-style helmets. I know this is a free country, but is that okay? So many ideas are whirling through my head that I feel a little dizzy.

I think about how terrible it is to hate so much. I know, because I used to hate the boys who caused the car accident.

When I stopped hating them it was like I stepped out from under a dark cloud and saw the sunshine again.

"My grandmother had to leave Poland because people there hated her since she was Jewish," I tell Joy. "And a lot of people here treat Mami like she's stupid because she doesn't speak English. How can people be so mean?"

"I don't know the answer," Joy says. "I wish I did. But I'm grateful for the many good people there are too, like Dr. King, who is trying to teach us to be tolerant and accepting of each other, so we can all live together in harmony."

"Or like José Martí, who'd give a white rose to his friend and his enemy."

"Right on, Ruthie, right on," Joy replies. Then she who has such a happy name speaks to me in a despairing voice: "But, Ruthie, I have to admit, the world can be a frightening place sometimes."

And suddenly the teacher I thought was invincible looks as if she wants somebody to say "there, there" to her, just like I often need someone to say it to me.

PART IV

Resting on the Point of a Star

one gold lamé sandal

When I wake up on Wednesday, December 21, I am happy that this year is practically over and that it's almost time to tear off the last month of the calendar.

It is also the day I am seeing Dr. Friendlich and I am hoping he will finally remove my cast, but I am scared too.

I have gotten used to my cast holding me together and I am afraid I might fall apart when it comes off. It's been so long that it feels like I may never walk again.

I am resting on the point of a star, far from everything I knew how to do before I broke my leg. Sometimes I wish I could shout to the world, "Tell me, please, won't you tell me? Do you know how to become whole after you've been broken?"

Mami is going with me to the hospital, all dressed up as usual, with no one to admire her and tell her how pretty she is, except me.

I'm expecting Bobbie and Clay to come for me, but two other men arrive.

They don't tell me their names and I don't ask.

I'm only outside for a few minutes. It's freezing and that makes me want to be back in my cozy bed. I feel sorry for the bare trees that have lost their leaves and are waiting for spring to bring them back.

Then I notice their branches are as fine as lace. I remember what Chicho taught me about perspective and all of a sudden the winter seems beautiful to me, a time of hibernation and waiting, just like I've been hibernating and waiting.

Dr. Friendlich is amused when he sees my painted cast.

"Sure you want me to take this off?" he asks.

"My neighbor Chicho took a picture with his Polaroid camera," I tell him.

"Oh, good."

He cuts and I watch, happy and sad, as flowers, butterflies, and birds fall to the floor.

After they take the X-ray, Dr. Friendlich stares at it for a long time. Trying not to sound worried, but looking worried, he says, "It's healing . . . but not as quickly as we'd like . . . Hmm . . . Let's not take any chances. I'm going to put a cast just on your right leg. Your left leg will be free, but I can't give you a walking cast yet. You'll still have to stay in bed. Maybe two months. If we're lucky . . ."

I watch as he creates a new cast for my right leg that goes from my toes to the top of my thigh.

"Here, Ruthie, sit up," Dr. Friendlich says. "Very slowly. Your muscles have gone to sleep, so you need to go easy on them."

My belly is free and my back is free for the first time in so long. I thought I would be so happy when my body cast was off, but instead I feel like a turtle that's lost half of her shell. I inch forward at my belly, pulling my back up, trying to sit. It takes all my strength. Dr. Friendlich holds me so I won't fall over.

I look down toward my legs, one out of the cast and one still in the cast. I don't recognize my left leg, my good leg. It's all furry.

"Why am I so hairy?" I ask Dr. Friendlich.

He smiles. "It's a result of all your body heat trapped inside the cast. And you're growing up—as fast as I feared! Good thing I put you in that body cast."

I'm not sure what the hair sprouting on my leg and me growing up have to do with each other, but I nod as if I know.

"You can move the left leg all you want. Remember, it's not broken. Just been sealed up for a while. The muscles will take a little time to reawaken, but they will. And you'll be tempted to get out of bed. Don't even think of trying to stand up. You're not ready yet. Is that clear, young lady?"

He looks me straight in the eye to be sure I've understood.

"Okay, Doctor."

I don't know what Dr. Friendlich is talking about. I've forgotten how to stand up.

Aunt Sylvia is peering out her window when the ambulance pulls up to our building. As the men carry my stretcher out of the ambulance, Izzie comes running to meet me, along with Dennis and Lily, and Aunt Sylvia follows.

They crowd around.

"I don't have a body cast anymore!" I tell everyone. "But I have to learn how to sit up again, like a big baby. Isn't that ridiculous?"

"Yippee!" Izzie shouts, "You're almost back to normal!" He and Dennis and Lily jump up and down.

"So can she walk now?" Aunt Sylvia asks quietly, turning to Mami.

Mami's voice is sad as she says to Aunt Sylvia, *"Todavía."*

That means "not yet."

Aunt Sylvia replies, *"¿Hasta cuando?"*

That means "until when?"

Mami shrugs. I see tears in her eyes. I'm sure they're not for me. They're for her. She has to keep being my mother, keep taking care of me—the daughter who's got a hairy leg and another leg that might never heal.

After we get back upstairs, the glum ambulance men drop me in my bed like a sack of potatoes.

Mami leaves the room and I hear her weeping in the kitchen. I call to her, "Come back, Mami, don't cry by yourself."

But she won't listen to me.

Will our lives go on like this forever—me always in bed and Mami trapped in the house with me?

No, no, no! I can't let that happen! I have to get better. I'm going to start right now by moving my left toes. As Dr.

Friendlich said, my left leg isn't broken. It's just fallen asleep after being in the cast for so long.

The toes are stiff, but after a while I can move them. Very slowly I start to move my foot. Twirl my ankle. It feels like I'm lifting a brick. But the leg is coming back to life.

"Mami, look! Mami!"

Finally Mami returns, her tears all dry, and she brings me an apple, cut up into neat wedges.

"Here, *mi niña*, you need something to eat. I'm sorry you had to wait."

"Mami, I'm going to get better. Please don't give up on me. Look, I can move my left foot again."

"*Ay, mi vida,* be careful."

"It's okay, Mami. Really. The doctor said I could move it all I want."

"But be careful, it's been in a cast for a long time."

"I will, Mami, don't worry."

The sadness in Mami's eyes makes me sad. But then I think of a great idea.

"Mami, please let me wear one of your shoes on my left foot, just to see how it feels."

At last, Mami smiles a true smile. "Of course, *mi niña*, of course."

She rushes to the hallway closet and comes back with a bunch of her high heels and lets me choose any I want. I select her gold lamé sandals, which have a thick platform sole and an ankle strap.

"Mami, put it on my left foot. Please."

My belly and back are stiff and achy, so I can't reach down yet to my foot.

"Now you put the other sandal on," I tell Mami.

"Why?" she asks.

"For fun," I say.

She slips the sandal on to her right foot and stands on one foot. She hops around before losing her balance and catching hold of the edge of the bed not to fall down.

"It's not easy to walk on one foot," Mami says.

"Mami, stay with me," I tell her.

"*Sí, mi niña,*" she replies.

She comes and stretches out beside me on the bed.

With one gold lamé sandal on my left foot and one gold lamé sandal on Mami's right foot, we're a complete person.

Dear Frida,

    I don't dare tell Mami or Joy that I'm not sure if I ever want to get out of bed. I can't say that out loud. They'll think I am crazy. I hope I'm not.

    Did you ever feel this way, Frida? That a part of you wants to be healed and returned to normal and another part wants to stay just as you are, quietly in bed, painting your pictures, safe from all the mean people in the world?

    Please give me a sign, Frida, if you understand me.

    I really hope I'm not crazy.

                         Ruthie

my Royal typewriter

After a few days I can sit up easily in bed.

My left leg feels fine, like it used to before the accident. I don't like its hairiness, but Mami says I am too young to shave. She still has to bring my meals to me on a tray, but now I can eat normal portions. I can even hold a plate up on my left knee. I kind of look like the god Shiva on my pendant, my right leg unmoving in the cast and my left leg on the loose. But I'm not dancing yet, that's for sure. And Mami still has to bring me the bedpan. We both can't wait for that to end!

To celebrate my graduation to a smaller cast, Papi says he's going to get me a typewriter.

"You're so smart, *mi hija*. When you grow up, I want you to become a secretary. They're always looking for girls who type fast and don't make mistakes."

He comes home with a used Royal typewriter for me to get started.

"But, Papi, I want to be an artist, like Frida Kahlo from Mexico," I tell him.

"An artist? That's not a good profession for a nice girl," he says, frowning.

"Don't you like my pictures?"

"I know Chicho has been encouraging you. But artists are always poor. You don't want to be poor, do you?"

"Papi, that's what Chicho's father told him! Because of that, he gave up his dream of becoming an artist."

"How about if you learn to type so you'll be able to support yourself? I bet you can learn to type a hundred words a minute like the best secretaries."

I figure it can't hurt to learn. Papi builds me a wooden stand with little legs, so I can set the typewriter on it and type in bed. He gets me an orange typing manual. I am to do one lesson a day. By the end of the book I'll be able to type with my eyes closed.

I quickly memorize the A-S-D-F on my left hand and the ;-L-K-J on my right hand and that makes Papi very happy. I know how hard he's working to pay back Dr. Friendlich. I feel bad he lost his blue Oldsmobile in the accident. He loved that car so much.

I want to learn to type a hundred words a minute. Maybe Papi is right. I should give up my dream of being an artist. I will become a secretary and make a ton of money and give it to Papi so he can buy a new car.

But if I do that, will I be sad my whole life?

Dear Frida,
    Are you listening?
    Say yes!

                    Your faithful,
                    Ruthie

I do the lessons in the orange typing manual and at first I'm really clumsy, but after a while I start to know the keys by heart.

Soon I can close my eyes and type the letters without looking at the keys.

But the lessons get harder and harder, and when I have to type out a whole page, I get lazy and want to give up.

Then I take a deep breath and keep typing.

I start thinking this typing thing could really come in handy someday since I like to tell stories. Maybe I can become a writer too. But I won't tell Papi. Being an artist *and* a writer will seem crazy to him!

One afternoon, when Mami needs to go out grocery shopping, Baba comes over to keep me company.

"*¿Té quiere?*" she asks.

I laugh and say, "*Sí, te quiero.*"

It's Baba's favorite joke in Spanish, a pun. The word for "tea" in Spanish is *té*, and when you say "I want tea," it's *quiero té* and when you say "I love you" in Spanish, it's *te quiero*, so my answer means both "Yes, I want tea" and "Yes, I love you."

Baba makes Lipton tea for the two of us. She sits next to me with a tray of tea and a bowl of her sugar cookies. She calls the cookies *kijeles* in Yiddish. They are jawbreaker cookies because they are hard until you dip them in tea.

We dip our cookies in the hot tea, and they soften and taste delicious. Then Baba takes a sugar cube and puts it in her mouth and sips her tea so it gets sweet that way. I can't even bring the cup of tea to my mouth. I have to wait until it cools.

While I'm waiting, I say, "Baba, how did you meet Zeide?"

She takes another sip of tea through the sugar cube before she replies. "I never told you that story?"

"No, Baba, I don't think so. I bet it was love at first sight."

"Not exactly, *shayna maideleh.*"

"Is it okay if I type your story? That way I can get better at typing."

"Be my guest," Baba replies and I smile. That's her favorite expression in English. Baba goes on, "So I landed in Havana and I found a bed in a rooming house for Jewish ladies. All I could afford were sandwiches made of bread and bananas. As soon as I heard they needed a saleslady at a fabric store in the old part of the city, I went running. It's all cobblestones there, and I was sweating when I got to the store. The man who needed the saleslady was your grandfather, your zeide. He asked if I could measure fabric straight, and if I knew how to add and subtract. I told him yes and he hired me on the spot. I worked hard that first day and the next and the next, and he gave me a raise. Suddenly I had enough money to go eat lunch at the Moishe Pipik restaurant. I had gefilte fish and matzo ball soup and an apple strudel for dessert, all the foods I missed from home. After two weeks, I could buy myself a new dress. And I was still saving money to bring over the family from Poland."

"Okay, Baba, wait a minute, I'm trying to type everything you're saying."

"Of course, *shayna maideleh*. I am in no rush. How can you type so fast?"

"You see, Baba, I'm trying to learn to type a hundred words a minute." And in a whisper I tell her, "I want to be an artist *and* a writer. But don't tell Papi. He wants me to be a secretary when I grow up."

"Your secret is safe with me," Baba says, dipping another cookie in the tea.

"*Gracias*, Baba," I say. "And then what happened?"

"Well, I kept working for the man who would one day became your zeide. After several months, he said to me, 'Will you marry me?' Just like that. I said, 'Do you love me?' And he said, 'Of course.' So I said, 'Yes.' And he said, 'I'm glad you said yes, because it's going to cost me a lot less to have you as my wife than as my saleslady.' It turned out he was paying me three times what a normal saleslady earned! He wanted to make sure I didn't go anywhere else! How do you like that?"

"It's a great story, Baba."

"So now you know how I met and married your zeide. We've been together ever since, through all the hard times

161

and all the good times too." Baba sighs and asks, "Don't tell me, did you manage to type all of that?"

"I got every word, Baba."

"Then you will be a writer one day, *shayna maideleh*."

I am so happy I hug my Royal typewriter. And then I say, "Baba, you have to keep telling me stories, so I'll have inspiring things to write about."

"Naturally, *shayna maideleh*. And perhaps one day you will tell my stories to people who never knew me. That way the stories won't be forgotten."

"I will, Baba."

"I know you will, *shayna maideleh*. You listen well and that makes you a good keeper of stories. I am sure that all my memories are safe with you."

the snowman

It's New Year's Eve and Mami is making a big flan with a dozen eggs for a midnight treat. I hear her in the kitchen, breaking the eggs into the bowl, and I realize now that I can sit up I could be helping her.

"Mami, bring the bowl here! And the eggs! I can beat them for you."

"*Mi niña*, good idea. I can be making the sugar crust in the meantime."

There are still nine eggs to break into the bowl. I am careful to beat each one until it's creamy yellow and then when I've finished beating all the eggs, I ask Mami to bring the milk and the vanilla so I can mix in those ingredients.

"Here you go, Mami."

"Now I'll pour it in the pan with the sugar crust and let that pan float in another pan filled with water and put it in the oven. We call that a *baño María*. So the flan won't burn."

Just before the clock strikes midnight, Mami brings in a big bowl of grapes, and she and Papi and Izzie gather around my bed. As we count down to the new day, we follow the Cuban custom of gulping down thirteen grapes as quickly as we can. It's supposed to bring good luck. And then we all say, "Happy New Year!"

A few minutes later, Baba and Zeide come to say "Happy New Year," and Uncle Bill and Aunt Sylvia and Dennis and Lily come to say "Happy New Year."

Dennis and Lily have party horns, and they blow them and make as much noise as they can. They jump up and down with Izzie and play tag, chasing each other around the room, until finally Uncle Bill says, "Quiet down, kids. I need to make a speech." He clears his throat, waits for everyone to pay attention. "Happy New Year, my dear family. Let's hope for only good things in this year that has just begun. Most of all, let's hope Ruthie will get out of bed and walk again. I want to see her playing hopscotch like she used to!"

He extends his hands and they all make a circle around my bed.

There are tears in Mami's eyes, Baba's eyes, Sylvia's eyes, Zeide's eyes.

Papi says, "Why is everyone crying? It's New Year's! Let's be happy!"

Then Izzie points out the window. "Look, it's snowing!"

The snow is coming down in fluffy flakes. We see it reflected in the glow of the streetlights. Snow. Snow. Snow. Slowly. Slowly. Slowly.

Everyone stares out the window. Wow, how pretty. It's the first snowfall of the season.

Zeide smiles. "Reminds me of when I was growing up in

Russia. I rode with Mother and Father and brothers and sisters in our horse-drawn cart. Every so often we'd get stuck in the snow. We'd stop to fix it and have a snowball fight, laughing and stuffing snow down each other's shirts until we got sopping wet, and then we'd push the cart and get moving. What days those were."

Aunt Sylvia says, "Being born in Cuba, we never saw snow. Then I married Bill and came to New York. It still seems magical to me, how that white blanket spreads over everything and the world becomes so calm."

Izzie turns away from the window and announces, "I want to make a snowman! Can we make a snowman tomorrow?"

"Yeah, a snowman, a big snowman!" shout Dennis and Lily, the two of them jumping round and round in circles.

Uncle Bill replies, "Maybe we'll make a snowman. But you kids have to behave."

"We will! We will!" Dennis and Lily respond.

Uncle Bill winks at Mami. "Aren't we going to get anything to eat in this house?"

Mami laughs. "I almost forgot," she says.

"Yeah, what about the flan, Mami?"

"*Ay, mi niña,* let me run and get it."

Mami is wearing her gold lamé sandals for New Year's and she goes rushing to the kitchen, returning with the flan, which has turned as bright and golden as her pretty sandals. Its dark sugar crust has cracked on top and the syrup pours down the sides and onto the platter. Mami cuts up the flan and everyone spreads out around my bed and eats happily.

"Now this is what I call a superb flan!" Uncle Bill announces.

Mami says proudly, "Ruti helped make it. She beat the eggs right here in her bed."

"Muy rico," Aunt Sylvia says. "You're a good helper, Ruti."

I get a normal slice of flan. Finally! How delicious it is, this concoction of milk and eggs and burned sugar. It tastes like Cuba, like a dream you can almost remember.

In the morning, we hear a knock at the door. It's Chicho and Mark. "Happy New Year!" they say to Mami and Papi and Izzie. They come into my room and again they say, "Happy New Year!"

They're bundled up in coats, boots, gloves, and ski hats. Chicho looks at me with that twinkle in his eye. "Where's your winter coat?"

"But you know I still have to stay in my bed, Chicho. This isn't a walking cast."

"I know all that, *mi cielo.* But Mark and I are taking you outside anyway."

"But how? I can't leave my bed. The doctor said so."

Mark takes off his ski cap and slips it on my head. "Fits you well!"

I pull off the cap and throw it back at Mark. "Stop! What's going on? Are you two making fun of me?"

"No, *mi cielo,* of course not," Chicho says. "Please, Mark, you tell her."

Mark twirls the ski cap around in his hand for a moment, then throws it in the air and catches it.

"Surprise! Ruthie, guess what? I have two very good friends who work at the same hospital where I work and they happen to think you're a very brave young girl. We talked about it and they decided to pop in and give you a special New Year's Day gift. They're going to take you out to play in the snow."

The two friends enter. Wait? What? How is that possible? I think I must be dreaming. But there they are. It's Bobbie and Clay!

Clay says, "Hi, Ruthie! Ready to go outside?"

And Bobbie says, "Got your coat? We've got the stretcher and we brought you a nice warm blanket too."

Mami slips my coat over my shoulders. "Have fun, *mi niña!*"

Izzie throws on his coat. "I'm going to tell Dennis and Lily!" he says, charging down the stairs as we reach the elevator.

The front steps of the building are slippery, and Bobbie and Clay carefully carry me down to the sidewalk where I used to play hopscotch in the old days. They open the back door of the ambulance and bring out the wheeled bed and slip me onto it and wrap the blanket around my legs.

Then Izzie comes racing over with Dennis and Lily. Mark and Chicho follow behind, carrying two big shovels.

"Should we get to work?" Chicho asks.

Izzie, Dennis, and Lily cheer, "Yay! Yay!"

Mark and Chicho pile up snow with their shovels, creating the torso. Izzie, Dennis, and Lily pat down the snow and shape the roundness of the face. In between, they throw snowballs at each other.

Izzie brings me a snowball. "Here, Roofie, toss it!" I hold the snowball in my hand, fluffy and compact, the flakes catching the sunlight. Then I let it go. I throw it into the air and watch it fall and dissolve into sparkles.

I am happy. So happy!

Bobbie and Clay clap for me. "Nice throw!" Bobbie says. And Clay says, "Yeah!"

They stay on either side of me, watching to be sure I don't slip off the bed. When I'm with Bobbie and Clay, I feel nothing bad will ever happen to me again.

"What do you think? That's going to be one heck of a snowman," Bobbie says.

"Glad I'm gettin' to see it," Clay responds. "How do you like it, Ruthie?"

"It's beautiful," I say.

But their kindness is even more beautiful. Should I tell them that?

"Bobbie . . . Clay . . . You guys . . . Listen . . . Thanks . . ."

Being outside again, seeing the snow so white and soft, feeling the cool air on my cheeks, thinking about Bobbie and Clay coming on New Year's Day just to carry me outdoors so I can enjoy the winter morning, I can't help it, I want to cry.

"Kid, listen, don't get sentimental on us," Bobbie says.

And Clay adds, "Darlin', now you listen here, we came today because we wanted to."

Chicho turns toward us, smiling from ear to ear. "What do you think, Ruti? Do you like our snowman? Want to give him a nose and dress him?"

Reaching into the pocket of his coat, Chicho pulls out a carrot. "How's this for the nose?" From his other pocket, he reaches for a ratty wool hat and scarf.

Bobbie and Clay wheel me closer to the snowman, and I reach up and put the carrot in the middle of the snowman's face and drop the hat on his head and wrap the scarf around his neck.

I remember Zeide's story about throwing snowballs at his brothers in Russia and I think, one day when I am old, I will remember this day and the love I felt, throwing snowballs at my brother and making a snowman while my right leg still slept in a cast.

We are all admiring our snowman, but it's starting to get cold; I'm shivering, and I know Bobbie and Clay can't be around all day.

A familiar voice calls to me. "Ruthie . . . Are you better now?"

She wears a light blue coat and a black beret. So sophisticated.

But I don't want to talk to her. She is not my friend. I have been bedridden for eight months and she only came to visit me once and ran away as quickly as she could.

"Hello, Ruthie . . . Don't you remember me? It's Danielle."

I don't pay attention to her.

"Bobbie, Clay, I think it's time to go upstairs. I'm getting tired."

"Sure, kid," Bobbie says.

Bobbie and Clay slide me onto the stretcher and just as carefully bring me back up the steps to my building. Izzie,

Dennis, and Lily follow along, drenched from playing in the snow and ready to warm up indoors.

Danielle stays on the sidewalk, standing elegantly beside our snowman. As Bobbie and Clay edge me into the building, I turn back and catch her eye. She nods and smiles at me. But I don't smile back.

the shell is inside me now

Joy brings me a new calendar for the new year: 1967. Before you know it, I've torn out the month of January, and then the month of February is so short it goes quickly. And now it's Monday, March 13. Time to go to the hospital and take another X-ray.

Dr. Friendlich lifts his bushy eyebrows and smiles for the first time ever.

"Finally! You've healed. You won't need another cast."

"Really? Are you sure?!"

Dr. Friendlich laughs. "Of course I'm sure."

I glance down at my right leg, which is not going to need another cast. I haven't seen it in ten months. It's as hairy as my left leg.

"The nurse is going to help you," Dr. Friendlich says. "You'll stand on your good leg. Let the other leg hang next to it. No weight on it. Want to give it a try?"

"No!" I say.

"Ruthie, you're going to have to start getting over your fear," the nurse says. She tugs at my left arm and hooks it around her right arm. "Now pull yourself to the edge of the bed and swing your left leg around."

I inch forward slowly. I'm a turtle without a visible shell. But the shell is inside me now and it's grown hard and crusty.

I can't get up. I can't. Can't. Can't.

Dr. Friendlich sighs. "Well, Ruthie, you've made it this far. Now you'll have to learn to walk all over again, like a baby."

"But I don't remember how to walk!"

"Ruthie, have faith. It will come back to you." Dr. Friendlich pats me on the head as he used to do. He writes some words down on my chart. "We'll give you crutches and send a nurse to your house who will teach you how to use them."

"What if I don't want to get out of bed?"

"You can be an invalid for the rest of your life. Is that what you want, child?" He looks at me intently, waiting for my answer. "Well?"

"I don't know."

"A little stage fright is normal. But after that, it's up to you, child."

Dr. Friendlich turns and walks out, the nurse following after him. Then Bobbie and Clay appear, taking big, happy strides, as if everything were suddenly perfect.

Bobbie says, "You see, kid? It took a while, but you made it."

Clay says, "We knew you could do it, darlin'. You're my hero!"

I don't know why Bobbie and Clay are congratulating me. I haven't done anything. I've just been lying in bed waiting for my leg to heal and now I don't know if I'll ever be able to get out of bed.

Even without the cast, Bobbie and Clay still have to carry me in the stretcher. Things don't feel that different from before.

Clay winks at me. "What do you say? We'll turn the siren on at full blast."

"Might be the last time we can get away with it," Bobbie adds, laughing.

"Sure," I reply.

But I'm feeling sick to my stomach as we go roller-coastering back to Queens. This time I'm the one clenching Mami's hand in the back of the ambulance.

Aunt Sylvia is waiting at the curb. She asks Mami, *"¡¿Ya?!"*

Mami replies cheerfully, *"Ahora sí."*

Finally yes.

There is a look of relief on both their faces.

Aunt Sylvia asks, "How long before she can walk again?"

Mami says, "We don't know. She's got to learn again and she's very afraid."

Aunt Sylvia nods. "And you'll have to be patient again."

Mami sighs. *"Ya lo sé, ya lo sé."*

I know, I know.

I listen to everything they say about me, but pretend not to hear.

Then Bobbie and Clay bring me upstairs to my bed as always.

173

"Good-bye, kid," Bobbie says. "Get strong and don't look back."

Clay says, "I tell you, one day you'll forget you ever broke your leg."

"I hope so," I tell them. "I'm really going to miss you!"

"Better to miss us than to be needing us again!" Bobbie says, and Clay laughs.

They gather up the empty stretcher, and a second later, they're gone.

Why is it that bad things have to happen so you learn there are lots of good people in the world?

Then there's a knock on the door. It's Chicho. He comes to the bedroom and says, "Hello, Ruthie, I'm so glad your cast is off. Now you'll learn to walk and everything will be all right."

"I'm afraid to get out of bed, Chicho."

"But you'll do it anyway, *mi cielo*. Have faith."

"Chicho, why do you look so sad?"

"I have to go back to Mexico."

"But you're not going forever, are you?"

"I don't know yet. You see . . . my father died, *mi vida*. He sat down in his favorite chair to read the newspaper and his heart gave out. Just like that. Now my mother is alone."

"Oh, Chicho, I'm so sorry."

I want to give Chicho something to console him and I remember the embroidered handkerchief from Cuba that Mami let me keep.

"Here, Chicho," I say, passing it to him.

"*Gracias, mi corazón,* it's sweet of you to offer me such a beautiful gift."

"It's from Cuba. The only thing I still have from Cuba."

"Oh no, *mi cielo,* keep it, then. I am grateful for your kind thought."

"I want you to have it. Please."

"Well, if you are sure."

"I'm sure, Chicho."

"*Gracias.* I know I will need it."

He holds up a corner of the handkerchief to his face and dries the tears that have formed in his eyes.

"This is only the beginning, *mi cielo.* I know I will shed many tears when I get to Mexico. It's terrible I lost my father, but even more terrible that I didn't get to say good-bye. I left and came to America and didn't make peace with him. Now I don't know if my home is in Mexico or here."

"Chicho, didn't you say you love New York?"

"*Sí, sí,* I do, but there's so much to think about, *mija.* I won't know anything until I'm back in Mexico. It's the land of my ancestors. I need to set my feet down on that soil and see how I feel. I have missed my mother's warm tortillas and many more things than I can name."

"But you left Mexico to breathe free. Don't you breathe free here?"

"I am grateful for that freedom, but my roots are calling to me now."

"Promise me you'll come back, Chicho."

"I will try, *mija*. And I want you to keep getting better. Will you promise me you'll get out of bed and try to walk?"

"Okay, Chicho, I'll try."

But after he leaves, I fall back down into my bed and stare at the ceiling. I don't think I'm going to budge until he returns.

welcome back to the world

They send a nurse to teach me how to walk with crutches, but when she sees I don't want to get out of bed, she gives up on me fast. "I'm not going to force you. If you don't want to walk, then stay there."

The next nurse is nicer. "Honey, I know you been bed-ridden a long time, but you need to get up and try to walk. Come on, please try."

"I can't."

"Yes, you can. Let me show you. Please."

I feel sorry for her. I can see a tear in her eye as she leaves.

Mami is furious. "Aren't you tired of making pee-pee and poop in your bed?"

I am, I am, I am, I am, I am, I am, I am, I am, I am, I am.

But I cannot leave my bed.

I am scared to death.

Then the third nurse comes. Her name is Amara. She's from the Bronx and her family is from Puerto Rico. She has a scar on her cheek, from a street fight, she says. She's really tall. She towers above everyone. When she takes off her sweater, I see muscles on her arms.

"I hear you don't want to get out of bed, young lady. Is that right?"

"Yes," I say, my teeth chattering. "I'm scared my leg will break again."

"That's not going to happen. Not when you're with me."

She pulls away the sheets. I'm wearing a flowered nightgown that comes down below my knees.

"Let's start by getting you out of those pajamas or you'll never want to leave your bed. Where are your clothes?"

I point to the chest of drawers by the wall. Amara rustles around and chooses a few things and tosses them to me.

"Here, put on this blouse and skirt. Here's some underwear. Start getting used to wearing underwear again. Come on, put it on. It's not that hard. Lift up your hips and butt. You can do it. Use your arms. It's just a backward push-up. Stop acting so fragile. You didn't break an arm too, did you?"

After I'm dressed, Amara says, "The only way to deal with fear is to treat it like an unwelcome guest. If you keep entertaining it, you'll never be rid of it."

And then, without saying another word, she reaches over, picks me up, and flings me onto her right shoulder. She's so fast I don't even have time to be scared. A second later she sets me down on the floor, so all my weight is on my left leg, and she positions the crutches under my arms.

"I don't like this," I moan. "I'm all wobbly."

"You've been in bed for almost a year. Your muscles have

atrophied. What do you expect?" She looks at me with her tough boxer's gaze. "Stay there. Don't move. Get used to just standing."

"I feel like I'm going to topple over. Can I get back into bed now?"

"No, you can't. You're going to walk to the living room and say hello to your mother."

"That's too much. Please don't make me."

"Girl, listen to me, don't wear out my patience on the first day."

I'm about to start crying when I see her reaching for the crutches. She grabs them and tugs on them hard.

"Stop! What are you doing? I'm going to fall."

"Move your foot and you won't."

I hop forward with my left foot and catch up to the crutches.

"Keep doing that over and over again and you'll get there."

My left leg is weak, my arms are weak, and my broken leg, which they say isn't broken anymore, feels heavy, heavy, heavy.

But I keep on going.

Amara coaches me as if we were in the boxing ring.

"That's it. Crutches, and then leg. Keep up the momentum. Breathe, girl, breathe. You're not diving underwater."

Huffing and puffing, I make it to the living room.

Mami starts crying when she sees me. *"Mi niña, mi niña,"* she says. She hugs me so hard she nearly knocks me over, but Amara is there to catch me.

"Hay cariños que matan," Amara says, chuckling.

She speaks Spanish too!

"Así es," Mami replies.

And the two of them share a laugh.

"What does that expression mean?" I ask.

"It means there are loves that can kill you," Amara explains. "Your mother nearly tackled you to the ground she was so happy to see you. In other words, too much love can be a dangerous thing."

Mami pours steamy black coffee into one of her tiny cups and passes it to Amara. *"Un cafecito,"* she says, smiling.

Amara savors the coffee. *"Gracias, qué rico.* The sugar is just right." Then she turns to me and says, "Good work, girl. You've been standing there on your crutches for a good long time. Now I'll show you how to sit down in a chair and how to get up after you've been sitting. Then you'll get the rest of the day off."

Thanks to Amara, I can walk around the apartment, I can eat at the dining table, and I can finally go to the bathroom by myself.

But I still have a long way to go.

I can't go outside because there are five steps from the entrance of the building down to the street. I don't know how to go up and down stairs yet.

A few days later, Amara flings open the door of the apartment. "It's April," she says. "It's time you got some fresh air. Let's go out into the hallway. We'll learn to do steps here."

She points to the steep flight of stairs leading from our sixth floor to the fifth floor below.

At the top of the landing, she says, "You're going to lower one crutch down to the step below, slowly, and follow with the other crutch. Steady yourself. Then lower your left foot and let the right leg follow. That's all there is to it."

I look down and see the dark at the bottom of the stairs. It looks like a gaping wide dragon's mouth.

"I can't."

"Okay, let's try going *up* the steps first. It will be easier."

She presses the button for the elevator.

I dread it, but I follow her into the elevator and we go down one flight, to the fifth floor.

"Now, you'll set one crutch on the stair, then the other crutch, and you'll lift yourself up. Go ahead. I'm right behind you. I'll catch you if you fall back."

I do as she says. Crutches first. Lean forward. Hop up on my left foot and put all my weight on it.

"Wait! Did I do it?"

"Yes, you did, girl," Amara replies. "Keep going."

I go up another step! And another! And another!

It's when I get to the middle of the staircase that I'm scared out of my wits.

"Don't lean back, girl! You'll lose your balance. Take a deep breath. I'm right behind you. Keep going. Up, up, up. You're almost there."

When I reach the top, I feel I've climbed Mount Everest.

"I made it," I say to Amara. "But going down is still going to be impossible."

She smiles and the scar on her cheek twitches a little.

"Today it's impossible. Next week it won't be. You'll see."

But Amara is wrong. I can easily climb the stairs with my crutches, go up, up, up, but when I stand at the top of the landing and look down, down, down at the dark dragon mouth at the bottom of the stairs, my head spins like a top.

"Girl, I got you out of bed. Now I want to get you out of the building and into the street. Why do you make things so difficult?"

"I'm sorry."

I swallow the tears that slip down my cheeks. How I wish I were strong. How I wish I were brave.

"Look, I'll stand in front of you as you take each step down the stairs. If you trip, I'll catch you. Let me be your pillow."

I want to please Amara but the stairs are so steep and they go on forever. How will I balance on one foot and crutches? If I miss a step, I'll go toppling down and break my neck and break my back and break my leg and break my skull and be so broken not even Dr. Friendlich will be able to put me back together.

"Sorry, I'm sorry," I say, whimpering pathetically.

We are standing outside the door of the apartment. Amara's back stiffens, and she turns and presses the button for the elevator. When the door opens, she steps in, looking back at me angrily. "Okay, girl, you've worn me out. Go back to bed. I guess that's what you want to be for the rest of your life—an invalid."

The door closes shut and she's gone.

I collapse into my bed after Amara leaves. I only get up to go to the bathroom and to eat when Mami calls me to the table.

I'm going to stay in bed for the rest of my life. What's wrong with that?

There are lots of things I can accomplish in my bed.

I surround myself with all my books. I can do all my homework and get lots of gold stars from Joy.

I can type a lesson a day. I already type a hundred words a minute without having to go anywhere.

I can paint in bed like Frida Kahlo did. I just made a picture of a girl rolling down the stairs tangled up in her crutches. It hurts to look at, but it's beautiful.

It's amazing how much a girl can accomplish staying in her bed.

Wait till Amara comes back. I'll show her!

But I don't think Amara is coming back.

A few days later Amara knocks at our door. Mami gives Amara a *cafecito* in the living room. I hear Mami saying, "She's gone back to her bed. I don't know how you'll get her up again."

"All right, girl," Amara says, entering the room. "I gave you a break. Time to get back to work."

I pretend I don't care she's returned.

"I'm doing fine in bed. Look at all the gold stars my teacher gave me. And look at all the pictures I painted. And I can type a hundred words a minute with my eyes closed!"

"That's good, but there's a whole world out there waiting for you. Don't you want to touch the leaves on the trees? Feel the sun warming your back?" She opens her arms wide. "Come on, girl, you've got to get out of bed."

"Nah, I'm okay."

"How about friends? Wouldn't you like to play in the park with your friends?"

"I forget what friends are. No one comes to see me."

"Maybe they think you're upset with them. Anyway, listen, I figured out a way to make it easy for you to go down the stairs."

"I'll never go down the stairs. Never! If I slip and fall, I'll break like Humpty Dumpty into hundreds of pieces and then who'll put me back together again?"

"Listen to me, girl. You can go down the stairs. I'm going to show you how. I was so upset the other day I wasn't thinking clearly. I think your problem is vertigo. And we can take care of that. Come on, girl, please. Get up for just a moment."

I see the scar on Amara's cheek stretch as she winks at me.

"You must have been in a pretty bad street fight to get that scar."

"Yeah, it was bad."

"Can you tell me the story? I like stories. I'm going to type it up."

"Well, I always say it was a street fight so I don't have to go into the details of the real story. You see, it was a neighbor who did this to me. I was on my way home from school one day and no one was around. He stopped me and said it was his birthday and he wanted me to kiss him. 'Come on, just one little kiss. It won't hurt,' he said. When he tried to put his arms around me, I pushed him away as hard as I could. I watched boxing matches on TV, so I knew how to strike back. But then he took out his knife and left me with a memory of that day."

I finish typing just as Amara finishes telling her story.

"Wow! That's really scary, Amara. And now you have that scar for your whole life."

"We all have scars, Ruthie. Some of us have scars you can see and some of us have scars that we hide deep inside, hoping no one will ever ask about them."

She runs her fingers lightly over the scar and lets herself be sad for just a second. Then she says, "Now what do you say we stop talking and get moving? Ready to get out of bed?"

"Just for a little while, right?"

"Yeah. Come on, girl."

I follow her out the front door and we get into the elevator. She presses the button for the fifth floor. When we arrive, she says, "All you have to do is climb one step. That's it. Then stop. You think you can manage that?"

"Okay. Sure."

I do as she says. "Now what, Amara?"

"Turn around slowly. Pivot and turn your crutches around. That's it. Keep going until you're facing forward."

She stretches her arms out, so she can catch me if I lose my balance.

"It's just one step. Lower one crutch, then the other.

Put both crutches down on the step. Now lift yourself up. Steady, steady. Okay, now make a smooth landing on your good leg. That's it! You're there!"

"I did it! I did it!"

Amara lifts me into the air, with my crutches and everything, and gives me a hug. I notice she's sweating as much as I am.

"Now what do you say you go up two steps, then come down two steps?"

"Sure!"

I keep going, and do three steps and come down, then four steps and come down, then five steps and come down.

Amara says, "Let's stop there. Five steps are more than enough for one day. Want to go outside? It's five steps down to the street. Now you know you can do it."

We get back in the elevator and go down to the first floor. Amara holds the front door open for me.

"Ready to go outside?"

"I'm ready."

Amara watches as I make my way down the five steps. Crutches, then feet, crutches, then feet. Slow and steady.

"Think you can walk a bit?"

"Sure."

I'm shaking from the excitement. I'm outside!

Everything looks fuzzy—the cars whizzing by, the sun in the sky, the budding trees, the woman pulling a shopping cart filled with groceries. I rub my eyes. It feels like I'm dreaming.

Someone runs toward me.

"Ruthie, Ruthie!"

I know it's Danielle from her voice, but I can't make out her face until she's standing right next to me.

Danielle disregards the "Keep Off the Grass!" sign and pulls up a dandelion from the earth.

She hands the dandelion to me. Should I accept it? I was angry with her. But I'm too happy now to be angry.

As I take her gift, Danielle says, "For you, Ruthie. Welcome back to the world."

PART V

IF YOUR DREAMS ARE SMALL, THEY CAN GET LOST

true friend

Today is my one-year anniversary. A whole year has passed since the accident.

Joy says I should finish up the school year at P.S. 117 with my classmates in the sixth grade. "You'll fit right in. You've done all the same assignments, plus extra reading and math. And you can type a hundred words a minute. And you're a budding artist!"

Amara agrees with Joy. "Ruthie, you need to jump back into your normal life and go to school."

"Go to school? But how will I carry my books? I just learned how to go down the stairs. And I'm slow. What if the other kids grab my crutches? What if they knock me down?"

"Don't worry," Amara says. "I'll take you to school and ask for a volunteer in your class to arrive early and leave early with you every day. You'll have plenty of time to go up and down the stairs."

Mami buys me a white turtleneck to wear with a red jumper and a pair of sturdy saddle shoes. It's my first time wearing shoes on both feet since I came out of the cast, even if I still can't set my right foot down on the ground.

I rush to keep up with Amara on my crutches as we head to P.S. 117. Kids are running all over the place—in the yard, in the hallways. They look like spinning tops. If any of them bump into me, they'll knock me down.

I wish I could turn around and go home. But I climb up the stairs with Amara to the classroom. The other kids are already in their seats. Mrs. Margolis, the teacher, comes to the door and says, "Hello, Ruthie, welcome back. Please sit down." She points to a seat in front. Holding on to the crutches, I lower myself down, feeling everyone's eyes on me.

Amara announces, "Ruthie needs a volunteer to accompany her to school and take her home every day. You'll need to come to school early with her and leave school early with her, until the last day of school."

Mrs. Margolis opens her eyes wide and smiles at the students. "Who would like to be Ruthie's helper?"

She glances around the room. All the kids peer at their desks or out the window. No one wants to be a volunteer. I know why. The volunteer won't be able to play tag or jump rope with the other kids before or after school. They'll miss out on the fun because of the invalid who should have stayed in her bed.

One hand goes up. One very certain hand rises high up in the air.

"Teacher, I'll volunteer."

"Thank you, Danielle. Please trade seats with Mary, so you can sit next to Ruthie."

Danielle floats over to my side. I feel her hair lightly touching my arm as she sits down. A butterfly has landed on me.

That first day back in the classroom I take notes on everything Mrs. Margolis says. When she writes on the blackboard, I have to squint to see what she's writing. I keep looking over my shoulder at Danielle's notebook to make sure I'm getting it right. Danielle notices and edges her notebook closer to make it easier for me.

At a quarter to three, Mrs. Margolis announces, "Danielle, you may leave now with Ruthie."

Danielle stands, gathers my books and hers. I reach for my crutches and pull myself up. Everyone stares as we leave the room together.

As I hop along on my crutches, Danielle adjusts her speed so we can walk side by side. She opens the door for me when we reach the landing. I look down at the dark at the bottom of the stairs and feel a lump in my throat. We're on the third floor and I need to be on the ground floor before all the kids are dismissed.

I start my descent, crutches, then foot, crutches, then foot, crutches, then foot. Danielle stays by my side, taking a step at a time with me.

Finally I reach the bottom of the stairs and we hear the bell sound.

"Don't worry, we can make it," Danielle says.

Just in case, I hop along faster, extending my crutches as far in front as I can to take longer steps. My hands hurt from gripping the crutches so tightly. But I am happy we make it out to the street before the crowds of kids arrive, yelling and running and shoving each other.

Danielle walks with me to my building. She points to the building across the street. "Want to come over?"

"Sure. If my mother lets me."

I've never gone to another girl's house in America, unless you count my cousin Lily's house.

We take the elevator upstairs. Mami gives me permission to go to Danielle's house for an hour. Then Danielle is to bring me back.

"Is your mother at home?" Mami asks Danielle.

Danielle replies, "Oh yes, of course. My mother is waiting for me."

Mami looks at Danielle with curiosity. "I remember you are from somewhere else too. Is it France?"

Danielle says, "No, madame, I am from Belgium."

As we leave, Mami says to me, "Don't tire yourself too much the first day back in school. Be back in an hour like I told you."

"But I'm not tired!"

"You will be later," she replies.

Although Mami looks at me sternly, I can see that she's sad.

I say to her, "You miss me being at home with the bedpan? Wasn't that so much fun?"

"Don't be silly," she replies, and she laughs. "But, yes, some of it is true—I do miss being with you."

I know Mami is lonely. It's funny that now that I can go out on my own, she wants me home.

When we arrive, Danielle's mother, Mrs. Levy-Cohen, is in the kitchen. She's dressed in a fancy tweed suit as she stands over a pot of bubbling hot water.

"Come in, come in," she says cheerfully.

Danielle introduces me. "This is Ruthie. Remember you told me to visit her? She was in bed for almost an entire year with a broken leg."

Mrs. Levy-Cohen says, "Ooh la la! Poor child. But you are better, no?"

"Yes, much better," I say. "Thank you for telling Danielle to visit me. I was very lonely during that year."

"I told Danielle many times to go see you," Mrs. Levy-Cohen says. "All of us in the neighborhood knew how much you were suffering, Ruthie. Your aunt Sylvia told everyone. But we didn't need to be told. We saw you being carried back and forth in the ambulance. It broke our hearts."

Danielle lowers her head and mutters, "I'm sorry. I didn't like seeing you that way, Ruthie. You were Miss Hopscotch Queen. It wasn't fair. How could you, of all people in the world, end up in bed, not even able to sit up? It made me so sad. That day I went to see you, all I wanted was to cry and cry. That's why I didn't go visit you anymore. I would have made you more miserable."

"Did Danielle tell you what she did?" Mrs. Levy-Cohen says.

"Please don't tell her, Maman," Danielle pleads. "She doesn't need to know."

"But I will tell her, just so Ruthie realizes you had her

in your thoughts, even if you didn't go to visit her, as you should have."

"Maman, no, but if you must—"

Mrs. Levy-Cohen looks at me and smiles. "When Danielle heard you were in the accident and lost your go-go boots, she put away her go-go boots and said she would save them for you and give them to you when you were all healed."

"Come, I'll show you," Danielle says, and leads me to her room. The walls are painted dark pink, a grown-up pink, not a foofy pink. Her bedspread has a cool design of huge red and orange poppy flowers.

Danielle opens the door to her closet. "Look," she says. She shows me her go-go boots, nestled in tissue paper, resting in the box they came in. "Whenever you want them, they're yours."

"Thank you, Danielle. I thought you weren't a true friend. Now I know you are."

"I could have been better. But I promise I'll be better now."

There's a delicious buttery smell coming from the kitchen. Danielle looks at me, her eyes gleaming. "That's the puffs! Smells like they're ready."

"Puffs?" I ask.

"They're the best puffs in the whole world. Wait till you try them!"

Danielle's mother calls to us from the kitchen. "The puffs will be ready in five minutes, girls. Please wash your hands first."

"Yes, Maman. Of course."

Mrs. Levy-Cohen has set the table with two plates, two forks, and two lace napkins.

"Sit. Quickly! The puffs are at their best right now!"

Mrs. Levy-Cohen comes rushing out of the kitchen with a bowl of puffs. She places four on my plate.

I bite into the first one. I didn't expect it would be filled with cream. How did she get the cream inside the puff? It's magic. As soon as I eat my four puffs, Mrs. Levy-Cohen is waiting with another four puffs.

Danielle is happy I like the puffs so much. "I told you they were unique."

Mrs. Levy-Cohen laughs. "Danielle can eat a dozen puffs in five minutes. She's only eating them slowly because you are here. *Masha'allah, masha'allah.*"

"Excuse me, Mrs. Levy-Cohen, what language is that?"

"My child, that is Arabic. It means 'God bless you.' We say it to keep someone from catching the evil eye."

"So you don't get jinxed," Danielle adds. "Maman is always afraid of jinxing me."

"But you speak Arabic too? I thought you were from Belgium?"

"Let me try to explain," says Mrs. Levy-Cohen. "It's a long story. You see, *chérie*, I am originally from Morocco. I moved with my family to Belgium when I was a child. That is why I speak Arabic and French, and now English too, with my thick accent. It is Hebrew I should speak, because I am Jewish, but I never learned it."

She stands and begins to clear up the plates.

"Wait, Maman, can we have one more puff? Just one? Please?"

"You've eaten too many, but since it's Ruthie's first time, I will make an exception. But only for today!"

After being upset with Danielle, now I hope she will be my friend. I want to keep eating puffs at her house forever.

Yes, Danielle is now my best friend! Every day I go to her house after school.

Mrs. Levy-Cohen always has a surprise in store for us. She says we can't have puffs every day or we'll get so fat we won't fit through the door.

"Darlings, you must have healthy foods that won't ruin your figures."

She cuts up watermelon and little squares of feta cheese and runs a toothpick through them that has a tiny umbrella perched at the end. She gives us a warm bowl of tomato soup and I like it a lot more than I thought I would. She makes us cucumber sandwiches, the edges scalloped to look like flowers, filled with thin slices of salami. She slices a grapefruit and sets each half-moon before us with a special spoon that has prickly edges so we can tear into it. She mixes up frothy shakes out of cantaloupe.

Then it's time for puffs again. Danielle and I each eat a dozen. We feel like we've gone to the moon.

Mrs. Levy-Cohen makes Danielle and me so happy, but Danielle says her mother has had a sad life.

While we sit and do our homework together in Danielle's dark pink room, she tells me, "We came to the United States to get away from my father. Maman asked him for a divorce."

"Why?"

"My father was not a very caring father. And he was an even worse husband."

"What made him so bad?"

"He was always at the café or the bar, never at home."

"But do you miss him anyway?"

"No. I hardly knew him. Maman doesn't miss him either."

"Even though he's your father?"

"Better to have no father than a bad father," she says confidently.

"Your mother is so brave. You are too," I say to Danielle.

"Yes, we're brave . . . most of the time," Danielle replies, suddenly looking sad. "Last night I had a bad dream, though. Someone was chasing me in a dark alley. I crawled into Maman's bed and we cried ourselves to sleep."

That is how I learn that even Danielle, who is so sophisticated, and Mrs. Levy-Cohen, who had the courage to ask for a divorce, even they are sometimes afraid to be alive.

I get to shine in the smart class

On a Saturday afternoon, when Papi is working and Izzie is out playing, Mami sees me sitting up in bed, a book close to my face, and she says, "Talk to me. Let me hear your voice. You always have your nose in a book."

"Mami, please don't make me feel bad because I love to read."

"I'm sorry, *mi niña*. I'm a little jealous. How quickly you devour all those books, as if they were chocolate bonbons!"

"Books saved me during all those months I was in bed."

"I know, *mi vida*. But now that you're better, you have to enjoy life."

"Okay, Mami, I'll try," I say, starting to feel a little exasperated.

"Tell me, Ruti, what are you thinking about?"

"Everything's fine," I say, eager to go back to my book. "I've been missing Chicho. I hope he's doing all right in Mexico. Do you think he'll come back?"

"I hope so. He brings happiness wherever he goes. He's pure *alegría*."

"At least he can go back and forth to his country. Not like us; we can't ever go to Cuba again. Isn't that sad?"

"*Ay, mi niña,* we're getting too *tristonas.* Let me brush your hair," she says. "You have such nice curls now. And soon you'll be a young lady."

"Oh, Mami, not now."

My hair has grown out, though it isn't as long as it once was.

"Please," she insists. "Are you going to be angry with me forever?"

"I'm not angry. You can brush it."

Mami gently moves from my roots to my ends, smoothing my hair for an instant, until it returns again to its natural curliness, like Papi's hair.

"So tell me about the book you are reading that you never want to put down," Mami says.

"It's a book of Greek mythology."

"What's that?"

"Ancient stories about gods and goddesses who once lived on earth. I just read the story of the god Apollo and the nymph Daphne. Apollo adored Daphne, but she wanted to be free, to wander in the woods by herself. And he kept chasing her and chasing her. One day, he was about to catch her, and she called to her father, who was also a god, to do something so Apollo would leave her alone. Her father heard her cries, and as she ran from Apollo, she suddenly felt thick and heavy, her hair turned to leaves and her arms to branches, and then her legs turned into a tree trunk and her feet into roots. She became a laurel tree. Apollo was sad to lose her, but then he used his powers to make her a tree that stayed forever green, so she'd never die."

"That's a strange and beautiful story, *mi niña*, and you tell it so well."

"Mami, I want to be an artist, and maybe a writer too, when I grow up."

"Those are big dreams."

"But they're not impossible, are they?"

"In my time, women didn't dream so big. It was enough to marry and be a good wife and look after the children. Now it's different. But you still have to grow up. A mother needs to take care of you, for you to become a grown-up woman."

"Mami, I'll never forget how you took care of me. *Te quiero*, Mami. I love you."

I say the words in Spanish and English, so she knows how much I mean it.

"*Ay, mi niña,* I love you too . . . Did I say that correctly? My English is getting better, isn't it?"

"It is, Mami, much better. Now you can get around everywhere by yourself. And you can defend yourself in English, if you have to, right?"

"*Así es, mi niña.* That cashier at Dan's Supermarket, who always bothered me, I finally said, 'Leave me alone or I'll call the police!' Now he bows his head when he sees me."

"Yay, Mami! That's great. But can you and I still speak Spanish together so I don't ever forget it?"

"Of course, Ruti, *por supuesto.*" Her eyes gleam brightly, without the usual cloudiness of her tears. "I hope you realize how proud I am of you? Please say you won't love me less when you've grown up and become an artist and a writer."

"I'm glad you have so much faith in me, Mami! Don't worry, I will still love you when I am famous." I smile at the thought and then become worried when I glance down at the book on my lap and have trouble making out the printed words. "Mami, I haven't wanted to say anything, but I think something's wrong with my eyes. I'm finding I have to hold the book very close to my face to read."

"Oh no, *mi vida*, maybe you need glasses."

"That's the thing. I don't want to wear glasses. Then I'll be a girl who not only needs crutches but also wears glasses. Everyone will feel sorry for me!"

"Come on, *mi niña*, let's not think that way. If you need glasses, you will wear them and hold your head high."

Next day we go to the eye doctor and he asks, "Can you see any of the letters?"

I can only see the top two rows—the big letter *E* and the *F* and the *P* below.

"Your eyesight has deteriorated," the doctor says.

I tell him about my broken leg and how I stared at the ceiling for a long time and how I read two or three books every day lying in bed.

"That explains it."

I get grown-up glasses with black cat-eye frames that Danielle thinks make me look very sophisticated and after a few days I forget I'm wearing them.

With my glasses, I see cracks lining sidewalks, the petals

on dandelions, the iridescent mother-of-pearl buttons on Danielle's blouse, and all the words and sentences and math problems that Mrs. Margolis writes on the blackboard. I love my glasses!

Joy was right. Being in bed for a year gave me an advantage over the other students and school is easy for me. Now I get to shine in the smart class!

Each day in class Mrs. Margolis asks us questions. "Anyone know what this word means? Anyone know what book I've taken this sentence from? Can anyone tell me how to solve this math problem? Anyone know the capital of Utah? Anyone know the names of all the oceans of the world?"

Mrs. Margolis looks around the room to see who will raise a hand. She can count on me to always raise my hand. I raise my hand so much that Mrs. Margolis has gotten used to saying, "Anyone besides Ruthie know the answer?"

When I walk home from school with Danielle, she says, "Ruthie, one day you're going to be a teacher, you're so smart."

But as we pass the sidewalk where we used to play hopscotch, I grow sad.

"I don't know if I'll ever play hopscotch again, though."

"Of course you will, Ruthie!"

"You can play if you want to, Danielle. I won't mind. Really."

Danielle shakes her head. "No, *chérie*. I am your friend and I do not want to play hopscotch until you can play."

We sit down on a bench in the park next to our buildings, joining the old ladies who go to the beauty parlor once a week and protect their hairdos with hairnets kept in place with bobby pins.

Izzie, Dennis, Lily, and the other kids on our block play tag or toss a ball around. They've thrown their jackets and schoolbooks to the ground and are all chirping like little birds with delight.

"Danielle, go play."

"It's okay. I don't mind."

"I have an idea. Danielle, you go play and I'll draw a picture of you."

I have a notepad and some colored pencils in my bag and I start to draw. Danielle is so elegant that her hair stays in place as she runs. She's fast. The other kids can't keep up with her. And she's graceful, like a greyhound, so I draw her face and dark eyes but give her the body of that dog with long sleek legs.

Every couple of minutes, she returns to my side, looking concerned.

"You're sure you don't want me to be here with you?" she asks.

"I'm fine," I assure her. "Go. I can keep drawing."

She runs off but looks back to make sure I'm drawing.

When she's done playing, she comes over and I show her my drawing.

"This is for you, Danielle."

"Très jolie!" she says. *"Merci."*

"I hope you won't ever get tired of being my friend," I say.

"Of course not, *chérie*. We are true friends and that is for life."

The sun seems to shine so brightly as Danielle says those words to me.

you can't hug the wall forever

I hear Amara arrive. As usual, she has a *cafecito* first with Mami in the kitchen. Then Amara calls out, "Okay, Ruthie, time to get to work!"

I hop over to greet Amara, proud of how nimbly I amble about on my crutches. She reaches over and snatches the left crutch out of my left hand.

"Okay, you're done with that. Time to transition to just one crutch."

"Wait! Why do you always like to surprise me?"

"Because I know you pretty well by now, girl, and unless I catch you off guard, you won't try anything new."

"But I'm used to two crutches! It's not fair!" I wail.

"Girl, listen, all you have to do is balance on your left leg and on the crutch that's in your right hand. Now take a step forward with your right leg. That leg is healed. It's stronger than it was before you broke it."

"I can't."

"Yes, you can."

She darts toward me and grabs hold of my right leg and pulls it forward. In order not to topple over, I end up putting my weight on that leg, the broken leg.

"You did it, girl," she says. "Bingo!"

For a second I can manage. A second later I get scared. Amara slides a chair under me just in time.

"Why did you make me do that? I wasn't ready."

"Don't be angry at me, Ruthie. You took a step, your very first step. You're learning to walk all over again. Just like a baby."

After a week, I get used to being a three-legged creature.

Then Amara comes back the next time and says, "Give me that crutch. You need to start walking on your own."

"Please, Amara, not yet."

"You'll get too used to the crutch and it will be harder to wean you off of it. Let me see . . . Here, I have an idea." She stretches out her arms toward me. "Hold on. Pretend I'm a rope."

"I'm scared. I don't want to break my leg again!"

"Oh, girl! You have so many fears you could make a merry-go-round spin in circles for days. I know you've been through a lot. But trust me, you can do this. I won't let you fall."

I grab hold of Amara's strong arms, clinging for dear life with both my hands as she edges herself backward. I go skidding forward like I'm on a sheet of ice.

"Okay, it's a start. Take a rest and give it another try tomorrow when you wake up. Promise?"

"Sure," I say.

But next morning I reach for my crutch and don't let go of it all day. And the same thing happens the next morning and the next and the next.

Amara is disappointed in me again.

"I thought by now you'd have thrown that crutch in the incinerator."

"Please don't take it away," I beg.

"Sometimes you have to dive before you swim. I think you know that by now. Come, let's go out into the hallway."

I follow Amara out of the apartment. Suddenly she turns and snatches the crutch from my hand.

"If you want it, come and get it!" she declares and sprints to the other end of the hallway.

"Amara, give me my crutch!"

"Come on, kid, you can do it. Step by step."

On shaky legs, I inch myself back until I reach the wall. Leaning against the wall, I feel safe. I keep inching sideways until I get to where Amara is standing.

"Good start," Amara says, "but you can't lean against the wall forever. Leave the wall and walk over to me." She steps into the middle of the hallway and spreads out her arms. "Here, come here."

"Please. Not today."

"Girl, just try."

"I can't! I give up! I don't care! I want to go back to bed and be an invalid for the rest of my life!!"

I turn to the wall and spread out my arms, trying to hug the wall. Right then a door opens next to me.

It's Chicho!

"You're back at last. I'm so happy to see you!"

"*Mi cielo*, what's going on here?" he asks. "Looks like you're walking, how wonderful! Do you two want to come in? It's a bit of a mess in the apartment. I got back last night and just woke up. I'm still unpacking. I brought back beautiful things from Mexico."

"Chicho, I was beginning to worry you were gone for good."

"Ruti, I cried a lot in Mexico, but I decided to leave all my tears there and return to New York. My father left money for me. And I'm going to do what I've always wanted—go to art school. I'll start classes in the fall! Isn't that exciting? But, Ruti, look at you! No more crutches, right? *¡Qué bueno!*"

"Amara just took away my crutches so I'm sort of walking. The thing is I'm afraid to walk on my own. But I can walk if I lean against the wall."

Chicho smiles and winks at me playfully. "That's nice of you, *mi corazón*, to be such good friends with the wall. I'm sure the wall is very grateful for your friendship."

He makes me laugh when he says that. But I still feel upset at myself. "I need to be able to walk without using the wall. Why can't I be brave?"

"Everything takes time. When you put a seed in the ground, the flower doesn't sprout right away. It takes sunshine and rain and many months in the soil for the seedling to turn into a plant and for the plant to blossom. You are about to blossom. I have an idea. Would you come in?" And he turns to Amara. "You too, please."

210

Chicho throws open the door and I inch forward, leaning against the walls of his apartment.

"What do you think of my walls, *mi amor*? I painted them blue and green, like the colors of Veracruz, my hometown, which is next to the ocean."

"I like them, Chicho!"

"Now look up. What do you see?"

"Chicho, they're piñatas!"

"That's right, *mija*. I loved piñatas as a child. It was always the best part of all the birthday parties. So I thought why not have piñatas all around me? That way I can look at them all the time. I think they're works of art too, don't you?"

"Yes, Chicho, yes! Will you let me have one for my birthday?"

"Of course, of course. *Ándale*. You can have any piñata you like!"

"Chicho, what's that in the living room? Don't you have a sofa?"

"Those are hammocks, *mi cielo*. I decided sofas were too boring and uncomfortable, so I strung up hammocks. When friends come over, we swing ourselves around, and if we get tired, we can go to sleep as happily as babies."

He flips on the record player. "Listen to this."

The music comes on. A man sings in Spanish. He sounds like he's stuck in the rain and his clothes are soaked and he has nowhere to go and warm his bones.

"That's Carlos Gardel. Beautiful, isn't it? Tango."

"Why is it so sad?" I ask.

"The tango is music for those who are sad. The tango is music to help you cry. So you can let go of your sadness. Then you can be happy again."

"I don't want to cry. I want to be brave."

"I understand, *mija*. But crying can help sometimes. The tango is also a dance. Women and men embrace each other and they dance all night, as if time didn't exist."

He smiles and opens his arms. "Can I show you?"

"I don't know," I say.

Amara whispers gently, "Girl, trust me. Your leg is healed."

"*Mi cielo*, listen to your nurse. She wants only the best for you. Now, if you'll give me a hug, I'll give you a hug, and we can dance the tango," Chicho says. "You can even close your eyes, if you want. I'll lead you."

"Okay." I take a deep breath and step into Chicho's arms.

"Just follow," Chicho says. "When I walk forward, you go backward. And when I walk back, you go forward."

Somehow, with Chicho holding me, I glide like a swan. Am I dancing? Sleepwalking? I close my eyes, swaying to the rhythm of that sad music. Tears are slipping down my cheeks, tears that are a river, a river flowing into the sea that surrounds Cuba, and I'm a little girl again in the streets of Havana, lifted by the breeze into the air. The dark, dusty world departs beneath me; and I look down and see my body cast, gleaming white from my waist to my toes, the way it did when they first put it on me. But now the cast is my feathery bird's tail and I am using it to soar higher and higher.

The music plays, and I listen to the words in Spanish and translate them to English in my head, such sad words:

> El día que me quieras . . .
> Florecerá la vida
> No existirá el dolor.
> *The day you love me . . .*
> *Life will flower again*
> *There will be no pain.*

I don't notice when the song ends. I'm still floating in my dreams. I hear Chicho saying, "*Niña linda*, I'm going to let go of you, okay? All you have to do is pretend you have an invisible partner holding you up, and you'll see, you'll be able to walk by yourself."

Chicho lets go and I extend my arms and touch the empty space around me, imagining him still there. Slowly I move forward, I don't know how I do it, but my legs take me to the center of the room. Then I stop and look around, breathless, grateful, relieved, not holding on to anything, standing tall.

"Yay, Ruthie, yay!" Amara says, brushing away tears.

"Amara, don't cry! You're too tough to cry."

"You're right, girl, you're right. But even tough girls cry sometimes. Like Chicho says, we cry to get stronger."

Chicho cheers, "Bravo! I think this calls for a piñata right now. Why wait until your birthday? Here, *mija*, break this one."

He runs to the kitchen and comes back with a broom. I

213

reach up and hit the piñata. It's a rainbow in the shape of an eight-pointed star. I hit it with the force of my whole body and break it on the first try.

I'm expecting candy to fall from the piñata, but no, it's something light, like snow, except all different colors. Snowflakes like bits and pieces of rainbows fall quietly on our heads. It's so pretty!

"What do you think, Ruti? I filled the piñata with confetti! Isn't it nice?"

"Yes, Chicho! You're covered with the confetti! And you too, Amara!"

Amara laughs. "Girl, look at yourself in the mirror. You've got enough confetti to last you a year."

I turn to look at myself in the mirror that's hanging over the dining table and that's when I notice Chicho's altar. In the center of the altar is the picture I made of little Avik, now in a wooden frame. There's a candle glowing brightly next to the picture and a stick of sandalwood incense in the burner waiting to be lit.

I think Avik was looking out for me just now. Little Avik watched me take my first steps on my own.

I remember I'm wearing the necklace Ramu gave me. I never take it off. I rub it for a second and, under my breath, I say, "*Gracias*, Shiva, the dancing god, *gracias*."

the broken girl says thank you

"Walk back and forth," Dr. Friendlich tells me. "I need to observe your gait."

It's embarrassing to be watched while I walk back and forth.

"Hmm," he says as he peers at me over his glasses, his eyes showing concern. "Ruthie, I'm sending you to physical therapy to help you get over your limp. Three times a week. Sometimes that last quarter mile is the toughest. You see the finish line but you don't know how you're going to get there. But you've come a long way, Ruthie. I know you'll make it to the finish line."

"Thank you, Dr. Friendlich. I hope you're right. I didn't think so at first, but you've turned out to be the nicest doctor."

"Thank you, Ruthie," he says, smiling. "And I hope I'm right too. I did what I could to fix your leg. Now you have to believe it's fixed."

Can thoughts travel and reach even those who are far across the ocean? Dr. Friendlich told me I had to believe, and

Ramu told me to try to have faith. So I am thinking of Ramu when a letter arrives from India in our mailbox in Queens.

Dear Ruthie,

How are you? Have you recovered yet from your broken leg? I hope so. Maybe by now you are playing hopscotch again?

I won't pretend. The last few months have not been easy. We miss Avik. But we were able to bring his ashes to the Ganges and so we know his spirit is at rest.

Here in India we believe in reincarnation. That means Avik isn't gone. He lives among us, in the air, the trees, the stones, the red earth.

I have a lot of family in India, more than a hundred cousins. I have lots of other children to play with.

My mother doesn't watch over me here as she did in America. She trusts that someone will always look out for me, wherever I am. Maybe she has also realized that even if she guards over me like a hawk, terrible things can still happen, so she has loosened her grip and let me be free.

If you have a little time and feel like writing to an old school chum, send me a letter, please. I would just like to know that you are well. Write and say "I am well" and that will be enough.

Your friend,
Ramu

P.S. Every time I eat guava fruit here in India, I remember your mother's guava pastry that you gave me to taste once in the cafeteria. Guavas are so common here. But in Queens they seemed so rare—like water in the desert.

Dear Ramu,

It's funny, I was thinking a lot about you and Avik, and your letter came. Brain waves? Magic? I don't know. But I'm so happy you wrote to me. I've been wondering about you.

There's a very nice man from Mexico living in your old apartment. His name is Chicho. He has an altar where he keeps a candle for Avik and a picture of Avik that I painted. While I was in the cast, I started making pictures. When I grow up, I want to be an artist. The first picture I made was of Avik. I'll always remember his sweet face.

I also have started to write down stories and hope maybe I can be a writer too. My mother says I have big dreams. But I think if your dreams are small they can get lost, like trying to find a needle in a haystack. (I just learned this funny American expression!) When a dream is big, you can see it better and hold on to it.

I've almost recovered. I can finally walk on both legs. But I can't jump or run so I can't play hopscotch. I have a terrible limp. I seesaw as I walk. Like the old ladies in the park!

The doctor says the limp should go away, but it might take a long time. Or maybe I'll always limp. Until I stop limping, we won't know for sure if putting the cast on both my legs was worth it or not.

I've learned I'm a terrible scaredy-cat, Ramu.

Everything has been hard for me—getting out of bed,
learning to use crutches, going down the stairs, walking
again.

> *Your friend,*
> *Ruthie*

P.S. I still wear the necklace you gave me. I pray to Shiva,
and also to the god of my forefathers, and to Frida Kahlo,
who is the guardian saint of wounded artists. Some people
don't think you should pray to more than one god, but I
wonder how many people who say that have spent a year
of their lives in a body cast and then tried to get up and
walk again? Not many, I bet. So I don't worry too much
about what other people think. I am free to be me.

Dear God, Dear Shiva, and Dear Frida,

I am reaching out to all of you, first of all, to say thank
you for listening to all my prayers and also to the prayers
that others have made on my behalf.

You helped me survive a terrible experience. I know
that all of you helped me to get through it.

And I am so lucky to have my family, my friends, and
everyone who has cared for me.

I'm happy to be able to walk again. Even with my limp
and ugly shoes.

But please, God, Shiva, and Frida, it would be nice if
you could help me get over my limp. Between all of you, I
know you can pull that off.

I feel bad for Dr. Friendlich. He put me in a body cast so my legs would heal properly, and now he's disappointed to see me limping. So if you could please go ahead and work your miracles, Dr. Friendlich won't have to know that it was really you that did it with a little extra help from the saints in Cuba.

Thank you, thank you, thank you!
Ruthie

a new Ruthie

School is over, and Mami and I have a new routine of taking the subway on Monday, Wednesday, and Friday to the clinic on Continental Avenue. I must look funny limping alongside my pretty mother in my big old saddle shoes—the only shoes that feel sturdy on my feet. People stare, but I find that if I look back at them and smile, it surprises them, and then they have to smile at me.

At the clinic, I see others who are recovering from all sorts of injuries. There is the soldier who lost a leg and is learning to walk with a prosthesis. His name is Jimmy and he says, "Howdy, Ruthie." There's the factory worker whose hands were flattened like corn tortillas by a machine. She is trying to regain enough strength to be able to do simple things, like eating with a knife and fork. Her name is María, and she says, *"Hola, corazón."* There is the grandmother who slipped in the shower and broke her hip and is learning to use a walker. She is a sophisticated lady with silver hair freshly teased at the beauty parlor and manicured nails painted red. Her name is Lucy and she calls me "Ruthie dear."

Jessica, the physical therapist, makes me do lots of exercises. I have to squeeze a rubber ball between my legs. I have to lift weights that are tied around the ankle of my right leg. I have to lie on a table on my back with my feet planted down and lift my hips and make a bridge with my body.

I think Jessica is too beautiful to be working at a dreary clinic with rubber balls and rusty gym equipment. She has platinum blond hair and used to be a cheerleader in high school.

"Did they throw you in the air and catch you?" I ask her.

"Oh yes! And I could do shoulder stands and twirl around like a ballerina and stand tall at the very top of the pyramid of all the cheerleaders."

"I wish I could have seen you. You must have been amazing!"

"That was a long time ago," she says. She looks away wistfully for a moment as if she were reliving those days. "The years pass and things change. You're not the person you were when you were younger, so you better like who you are now. I feel good helping people who are going through a dark time in their life."

She smiles big huge smiles, claps, and jumps when I make a little progress. She's always yelling out, "Hip, hip, hooray!"

But my limp doesn't go away.

"You'll get there," Jessica says. "Don't lose hope."

Every time she says that, I nod and remember the words from one of my favorite Emily Dickinson poems: "'Hope' is the thing with feathers / That perches in the soul."

I see a lot of hope at the clinic.

I see hope as Jimmy takes a shaky step with his prosthesis.

I see hope as María struggles to hold a fork in her flattened hands.

I see hope as Lucy shuffles along on her walker.

"Bye, Jimmy! Bye, María! Bye, Lucy!" I say as I leave the clinic. "See you next time!" And they smile and look at me with eyes that know we belong to the same club. We are the wounded of the world. But we know we are lucky to be getting help.

After I'm done at the clinic, Mami takes me to my favorite place. We cross Queens Boulevard, not rushing, stopping at the center island and waiting for the next green light, terrified of the racing cars. Finally we get there.

Nestled behind two old maple trees is the public library. I never know what treasures I'll find there. I love the old sign in the library that greets us: "Sing Out for Books." It shows kids reading books atop a big book of stories, flying as high as the moon.

Each week I pick up more art books, storybooks, poetry books, and anything that strikes my fancy. The books are heavy and Mami offers to help. But I feel like I should carry my own books.

When we get back to the neighborhood, Ava and June are playing hopscotch. Danielle stands there watching. She has been so faithful and kept her vow not to play hopscotch until I can play.

She smiles when she sees me coming. She has on a pretty flowered dress, perfect for the sunny summer weather.

"I'll come back down in a little while," I tell her. "I need to drop my books off and I'm a little tired from the physical therapy."

"Sure, Ruthie, I understand. I'll wait for you."

I go upstairs with Mami and sit down in the chair by the window in the living room where I like to read. There I can look out at what's happening in the street, while feeling safe at home. I want to start one of my new books, but I see Ava and June have left. Danielle is standing alone at the edge of the hopscotch board, waiting for me.

I tell Mami I'm going outside.

"Good, *mi niña*, get some fresh air," she says.

Going down the five steps from the building to the street, I remember the first time I descended those steps after all the months being an invalid, both legs shaking, my hands trembling as I gripped the crutches. And there stood Danielle, greeting me with a dandelion.

Now the lawn is green again and full of humble yellow dandelions. The sign is still there that says: "Keep Off the Grass!" I don't hesitate. I slip my hand through an opening in the fence, reach in, and pull a dandelion from the earth.

I bring it to Danielle and say, "Here, for you."

Danielle understands the meaning of this gift and she smiles and says, "So will you try to play hopscotch? Just take one step?"

"All right, Danielle," I say, surprising myself.

I watch as Danielle hops across the board, as graceful and light as always.

When she's done, Danielle says, "Now it's your turn."

"Please don't make me."

"But you said you would, Ruthie. Come on, nobody's here but you and me."

"I can't jump yet, Danielle. That's the problem."

"All right. Then just walk across . . . for old times' sake."

"Okay, just for you."

I'm excited and afraid as I step on the hopscotch board.

I set my feet inside the boxes and prepare to move from end to end. I recall the girl who could do this so easily, who could bound her way down the board feeling confident that her legs would hold her up. Now this is a difficult task. I must think about every step.

Slowly, carefully, I limp across the hopscotch. I look up and see Danielle smiling at me. I want to please Danielle. I think I can hop forward just on my left foot. But I stretch too far and lose my balance. "I'm going to fall!" I yell. Danielle stretches out a hand just in time, and I grab it and keep from toppling to the ground.

Danielle cheers, "Bravo, Ruthie! You see, you can do it! With practice, you'll get better, and you'll be Miss Hopscotch Queen of Queens again."

"Thank you, Danielle. But I'm never going to be Miss Hopscotch Queen of Queens again."

"Don't say that, Ruthie."

"Danielle, I'm a different Ruthie now. I've been through a metamorphosis. Now I am a girl who reads books and makes pictures. I like to be still. I like quiet. I can't go back anymore and be the old Ruthie. That Ruthie is gone forever."

When I see tears in Danielle's eyes, I take her hand and tell her, "Danielle, I'm so lucky you'll be my true friend always."

I see Danielle breathe a sigh of relief. "Come, let's go to my house. I will ask Maman to make some puffs for us to celebrate the birth of the new Ruthie."

Seeing me coming in the door, Mrs. Levy-Cohen exclaims, "It's always wonderful, *chérie*, to see you walking!"

"But I still have a limp," I mumble.

"That shall pass," she replies, waving her hand. "The less you think about it, the faster it will go away." And she smiles. "So you girls would like some puffs?"

"Yes, yes, yes!" Danielle and I reply eagerly.

We eat our puffs—a heavenly dozen—and then Danielle takes me to her pink room and pulls the black go-go boots out of the closet.

"Try them, Ruthie," she says.

"But it's summer. Let's wait until winter."

"No, try them now, to see if you like them."

I sit on the edge of Danielle's bed and remove my clunky saddle shoes. I slip on Danielle's boots. They are made of the softest leather. I zip them up and feel the boots hugging my legs very gently. My feet feel as if they'd sunk into the silky sand of Little Cow Beach in Cuba.

I stand up in the cautious way I've learned to move. But I feel so good in the boots, my body relaxes, and without thinking I place equal weight on both feet.

Danielle smiles. "I think they fit you perfectly, Ruthie. You look very nice, very chic! They go well with your glasses and your books! Why don't you walk in them and see how they feel?"

I step forward first with my left leg, my good leg, as I'm accustomed to doing. My right leg, my bad leg, follows. But as I take the next step, and the next, something unexpected happens. Suddenly I trust my broken leg! I've been putting all my weight on my left leg, trying to protect my right. That's why I've had a limp.

I keep on walking in Danielle's boots. I feel like I could walk to the end of the world and back.

Danielle claps and starts singing:

> *These boots are made for walkin'*
> *And that's just what they'll do . . .*

"Let's go show my family I am learning to walk normally again!"

Mrs. Levy-Cohen claps her hands too as we go out the door. "You see, *chérie*, didn't I tell you? Everything passes, the good and the bad."

When I ring the bell and Mami sees me in the boots, she says, "Ruti, whose boots are you wearing?"

"They're Danielle's boots. They're a gift to me."

Danielle says, "Look at Ruthie walk! Look!"

And I come into the apartment, walking with so little a limp that only I notice it.

"Mi niña, mi niña," Mami yells, laughing and crying at the same time.

Izzie comes home and sees the commotion. "What's going on here?" he asks.

"Your sister isn't limping anymore. Look!" Mami says.

I take a few steps back and forth to show him.

"Wow, Roofie! I'm going to tell Baba and Zeide!"

He rushes down the stairs and in minutes he comes back upstairs in the elevator with Baba and Zeide, who have just gotten home from Super Discount Fabric, bits of thread and lint clinging to their clothes.

And just then Papi comes home. *"¿Qué pasa?* Why is everyone here?" he asks. He sees me in Danielle's boots and says, "Where did you get those boots? I didn't give you permission to wear black boots."

"Papi, wait, don't get angry," I say. "These are Danielle's boots and something magical happened when I put them on. Look, I can walk again, without limping."

I walk a few steps. Papi and everyone watch me and then they let out a gasp like they've all come up for air at the same time.

"Dios mío, at last!" Papi says. He wraps his arms around me and Mami does too. Then Baba and Zeide kiss each other, whispering, *"Ay qué bueno, qué bueno."* And Baba sighs and says, "Now I will be able to sleep at night again."

I notice Papi has a package in his hand.

"What's in that box?" I ask.

He smiles. "A gift for you. But maybe you don't need it."

I open the box and pull aside the tissue paper. There they are: a pair of new white go-go boots, shiny and bright like two moons.

I look at Papi and he smiles at me again and nods.

I turn to Danielle. "These boots are for you . . . Do you like them?"

"I love them! They are *très jolie*," she says, and slips them on.

The boots fit Danielle perfectly. She floats in them like an angel.

I think about how Danielle and I are decked out in boots as though it were the winter, reminding us there will be cold, dark days ahead. But for the moment, life cannot be more beautiful.

We hook elbows, like two Rockettes, and Danielle and I belt out our song:

> *These boots are made for walkin'*
> *And that's just what they'll do . . .*

Within minutes the doorbell rings. It's Chicho! He heard us all from down the hall.

"*Qué amigos más falsos,*" he says, shaking his head. "How can you have a party and not invite me?"

"The party just started, Chicho," Mami reassures him.

"Ruti is walking without a limp! It's the boots that Danielle gave her. They're magical."

"What wonderful news! I knew this day would come. Let me bring something for the party. Ruti, would you like a piñata?"

"Oh yes, Chicho! Yes!"

That's enough to send Izzie running down to tell Dennis and Lily. Before you know it, they arrive, panting up the stairs, Uncle Bill and Aunt Sylvia following behind in the elevator. When they see me walking so easily, Aunt Sylvia sheds a tear and Uncle Bill proudly says, "That doctor didn't fiddle around. I told him to fix you up like new. And he did."

Chicho brings the biggest piñata he has in his apartment. It's in the shape of a heart, red tissue paper on the inside and pink tissue paper on the edges.

"I was saving it for Valentine's Day, but that's months away, and anyway I think this is a much better occasion," he says.

"I wanna break it!" Izzie says.

"Me too!" Dennis shouts.

"And me!" Lily shouts after him.

"I'd also like to give it a try, if I may," Danielle says politely.

"You'll all have a chance to break it," Chicho says.

One at a time, he blindfolds Izzie, Dennis, Lily, and Danielle and spins them around and around, so they are facing the wrong direction and totally miss the piñata.

Finally it's my turn. I let Chicho spin me around and

around. I know he will place me in front of the piñata so I can be the one to break it.

I give the piñata a strike with the broom, and sure enough, I hit it on the first try.

The paper heart comes undone, releasing its multicolored confetti over all of us like soft summer rain.

I lift my palms to catch the confetti and something I can't describe lands on me.

Is that what it feels like to receive a blessing?

It must be. For I was once a broken girl. And I'm not broken anymore.

I am lucky, after all.

One day I may even go on the journeys I dreamed of. People will say, "Look at her, she spent a year in bed, and now she travels far and wide." But wherever I go, I know I will feel most at home with the wounded of the world, who hold their heads up high no matter how broken they may seem.

I tear off the blindfold and watch the last bits of confetti pour out of the paper heart and fill the air with happiness.

But wait! What's that sound?

Music from Cuba . . .

Cha-cha-cha, qué rico cha-cha-cha . . .

Everyone is dancing and I am dancing too. It's so easy in the magical boots. I am light on my feet and feel like I am a little girl in Cuba again, lifted by the breeze, way up to the sky.

And what's happening now? My real heart, why does it hurt?

I think it wants to break open too.

That must be my heart's way of making room for all the love the world still has to give.

THE END

Author's Note

the grown-up Ruth remembers Ruthie

Many years ago, I wrote an essay, trying to tell the story of my childhood accident from the point of view of the grown-up woman looking back at the broken girl I had once been. It was not easy to tell the story. I cried as I wrote. Then it was finished and I thought, "Oh, good, I'm done with that story." I sighed with relief and moved on. But really I had barely begun to tell it.

Someone—I don't remember her name—read the essay and liked it so much she asked to speak to me on the phone. And she said to me, "Why don't you tell the story from the girl's perspective?"

She was right. Ruthie needed to speak for herself.

When I sat down to write *Lucky Broken Girl*, my childhood memories of being in a body cast for close to a year came flooding back. These memories didn't arrive as a coherent whole, but in bits and pieces, like pottery shards. Initially this book was a kaleidoscope of vignettes. I hoped

I might find some documents from that time to enrich the story. I remembered we kept one of the white plaster casts stashed in a closet for years, but then we moved to a different apartment and it got discarded. My mother likes to create albums of old family photos, so I asked her if there were pictures of me in the cast. "No, of course not," she replied, horrified I'd asked. They had not wanted to take any pictures of me in that condition, she told me.

This was a story I was supposed to forget. But I trusted my memory. And I did find the front-page story in the *Daily News* about the car crash. But most of all, I trusted the truths my body told me. This story is etched into my physiology, my nerves, and my many fears. It's what they call trauma. All those who've been wounded know what I mean. Maybe all who've been wounded are told, as I was, "It could have been worse." In other words, don't ask for too much sympathy. I remember feeling as a child that it was wrong to talk about my pain. Wrong to feel any pain. I buried the pain inside, where only I could feel it piercing me.

It took fifty years for me to release that pain and to honor the voice of the broken girl. I feel blessed to have found the words to tell this story, though I don't recommend that anyone wait that long. Pain is pain. Speak up. Tell your story.

But not everything happened exactly as I tell it here. I needed to let my imagination soar. There are things I wish had occurred in the fairy-tale way I tell them in this book. My bed was never turned around, and I yearned desperately to look out a window that year I was in bed.

Yes, I was in the dumb class. And yes, we had just arrived

in New York as refugees from Cuba when the car accident took place. We were scared. We didn't have money. We didn't speak English. We didn't know if they'd ship us back to Cuba. And if we had to flee again suddenly, what would become of me? I was immobile, a girl confined to her bed.

I seemed to take forever to rise up and walk. When finally I could walk, I seemed to take forever to stop limping. Healing is a journey and it takes its own sweet time. What a gift it is to get a second chance at life when the worst is past.

Throughout this ordeal, many good people tried to help me. I know I exasperated my family, but they loved me and watched over me as best they could. Most of the responsibility for my care fell on my mother's shoulders. I understand now what a burden that must have been for her. I had a loyal friend, Dinah, on whom Danielle is modeled, who really was from Belgium and introduced me to cream puffs. I remain grateful to my New York public school for sending a teacher to the house so I would not fall behind, an intense learning experience that made me a reader for life, and a writer. And Dr. Friendlich was a doctor who cared. While writing this book, I wanted to send him a personal thank-you for all he did for me, but I learned he had passed. I used his real name to honor him in this story.

Ruthie continues to live in me, the grown-up Ruth. You might not believe me when I say this, because I became a woman who is always traveling, a restless woman who lives with a suitcase by the door. But every now and then, if I fall ill with a fever or if I am hurt by someone's cruel words, if I feel weak and defenseless because the world feels too big for me, I become small again, and I crawl into my bed. And then, I have to tell you the truth: It's very hard, very, very, very hard for me to get up again. I become the girl in the cast, the girl in the white plaster cast. But I know that if the broken girl is cared for, she will stop being afraid. So I am patient when Ruthie reemerges, when she comes back to say hello. I lie there quietly listening to her fears, her sorrows. Then I tell her good-bye, muster my strength, rise and open the door and let the sunshine in. I become the grown-up Ruth and return to the world, no longer feeling so small. I step out, legs trembling a little but my heart full, and set forth on the next journey, entrusting myself to the beauty and danger of life all over again.

Acknowledgments

My first novel is a novel for children, and this is how it needed to be. As an immigrant child and a wounded child, I was forced to grow up quickly. I didn't get a chance to be a young girl for as long as I wanted. Writing this book gave me permission to return to my youth and reexperience that time, and even better, it has allowed me to make my childhood a bit happier than it really was.

I would never have gotten to this point if not for the kindness and generosity of those who believed in *Lucky Broken Girl* and urged me to give it my all.

I am grateful for all the wonderful writer-friends in my life. Ann Pearlman, my amazing writing buddy; Marjorie Agosín, a beautiful poet of the soul; and Rosa Lowinger, a dazzling fellow Jubana, were my earliest readers and rooted for me when this book was but a collection of fragmented memories. Rolando Estévez insisted I translate the book into Spanish while it was only a draft so he could read it, and he showed great *cariño* for me and my story by creating watercolor illustrations that let me visualize the characters and the setting. Sandra Cisneros was the tough-love *madrina* of this book, inspiring me with her writing and pushing me to make my writing better than just good. Richard Blanco's encouragement of my poetry and creative writing throughout the years has been a huge gift. And the words of support from Margarita Engle as I finished the book meant so much.

My agent, Alyssa Eisner Henkin, believed in *Lucky Broken Girl* from the start, and her unwavering faith in the story and in my abilities gave me the confidence I needed to write from the heart. I am deeply grateful to have had Alyssa as my guide into the world of children's literature. It was a real thrill when Nancy Paulsen chose *Lucky Broken Girl* for her imprint. I love all her books and dreamed of working with her. Nancy read my work with compassion, as if it were her story too, and her suggestions helped make this book a thousand times stronger. Thank you both so much.

I also wish to thank Joyce Sweeney for a manuscript critique that gave me important tools for plotting the story. Thanks to Sara LaFleur and the team at Penguin Random House. And thanks to Penelope Dullaghan for the gorgeous cover.

My husband, David, read several versions and always said they were wonderful, providing the unconditional support I think I don't need but know I do. And my son, Gabriel, who had to confront a leg injury of his own when he was growing up, read the book at the beginning and at the end and gave me his blessing, which I am so glad for. Thank you, David, and thank you, Gabriel; you have my love always.

Last but not least, there is a girl named Arianna who read

an early draft and gave me very thoughtful comments. She was nine then and already a serious reader. Arianna told me she liked the story, but it needed a few touches here and there for it to become a book. She was right, and the book grew as a result. As I wrote and rewrote, I never lost hope. I knew there had to be other young readers like Arianna who read to live and live to read, assuring me that reading is one of our greatest human treasures, to be passed on from generation to generation, so the world might be a better place for everyone.

About the Author

Ruth Behar was born in Havana, Cuba, grew up in New York, and has also lived in Spain and Mexico. The first Latina to win a MacArthur "Genius Grant," she is the Victor Haim Perera Collegiate Professor of Anthropology at the University of Michigan and received an honorary doctorate in Humane Letters from the Hebrew Union College–Jewish Institute of Religion. She has given lectures, talks, and readings at universities, cultural centers, book fairs, and bookstores, and she has been invited to speak about her writing in Spain, Israel, Japan, Italy, Ireland, New Zealand, Belgium, Mexico, Argentina, and Cuba.

As a cultural anthropologist, Ruth brings her heart into all her writing. Her notion of "the vulnerable observer" is one of the most referenced ideas in contemporary social thought. But she has always been a creative writer first and foremost, looking for ways to share ideas about cultural diversity and the search for home, inviting others to share the journey into the heart of the human experience.

Ruth is always in search of exciting ways to blur the line between memoir, creative nonfiction, and fiction. She is the author of several books that have become classics: *A Translated Woman: Crossing the Border with Esperanza's Story* tells the story of her friendship with a Mexican street peddler; *The Vulnerable Observer: Anthropology That Breaks Your Heart* is a personal voyage into the heart of the anthropologist who cannot observe others without feeling deeply for them; *An Island Called Home: Returning to Jewish Cuba* is the story of Ruth's journey home to Cuba and her search for the life she might have lived had her parents chosen to stay on the island; *Traveling Heavy: A Memoir in between Journeys* is about what it means to be both an immigrant and a traveler, offering a new way to think about the things we carry with us as we move about the globe.

Ruth is the editor of the pioneering anthology *Bridges to Cuba/Puentes a Cuba*, which brings together stories and poems by Cubans on and off the island. She is coeditor of *Women Writing Culture*, which has become a crucial resource on women's literary contributions to anthropology. Her personal documentary, *Adio Kerida/Goodbye Dear Love: A Cuban Sephardic Journey*, distributed by Women Make Movies, has been shown in festivals around the world.

Ruth's poetry is included in *The Whole Island: Six Decades of Cuban Poetry* and *The Norton Anthology of Latino Literature*, among other major collections. Her short story "La cortada" is included in the anthology *Telling Stories: An Anthology for Writers*, edited by Joyce Carol Oates. And, together with poet Richard Blanco, she has launched a blog, www.bridgestocuba.com, to create a forum for Cuban stories that engage the heart as the island moves into a new era of its history.

Visit Ruth at www.ruthbehar.com.